HOMEWARD

To James J. Whelan who has left this planet.
Inspirational, forever friend.

Homeward

Angela Byrne

MARTELLO

HOMEWARD
First published in 2017 by
Martello
An imprint of Brookside Publishing Services
16 Priory Hall Office Park
Stillorgan
County Dublin
Republic of Ireland

Print ISBN: 978-1-9998968-0-5
Kindle ISBN: 978-1-9998968-1-2

British Library Cataloguing Data: A CIP catalogue record for this book is available from the British Library.

Typeset by JVR Creative India
Cover design by Martello

This is a work of fiction. The characters in this book are fictitious and any resemblance with any real person is coincidental and unintended.

1.

*E*arly in 1916, with a long journey behind him and nostalgia and wonder in his heart, Richie Fitzgerald strolled up the lane towards the big house. The lane was rough, interrupted by stones sticking up from the soil. Watching his step, he rounded the corner in the bend, and stood still to allow himself to take in the view. He took a deep breath of fresh air, imbibing the smell of the grass, the chatter of the birds in the air and the beautiful scenery of the mountains in the distance. Everything was so quiet he could almost hear himself think. He had never witnessed such a quiet and peaceful setting before.

He wore a broad smile on his face, and sported a well-tanned face and neck. It was unusual for this time of year, in this part of the world. A fine and handsome man according to most women that knew him, no one would deny his good looks. Some of his friends back home likened him to the famous Kennedy-Fitzgerald family in Boston, USA. Richie would smile broadly when friends reminded him of his good looks and say, 'I get the good looks from my mother; my father didn't get a look in.' He had a way of standing and moving that commanded respect from people, but he was a gentle soul with a big heart.

There were six or eight cattle grazing in field on his right-hand side, flanked by a heavy ditch full of briars, nettles and weeds, which needed cutting back. It was incomparable to Boston, where life moved at a decidedly different pace. Nor was there any comparison with Cape Town, or with Port Natal in South Africa. It was like being in another world.

He had gone to South Arica to invest in the gold mines there. The Kimberley mines were turning up more gold than any other mine, and proved to be a good investment. His father was a wealthy man and had many investments in America, which were yielding great amounts of money. So he asked his only child to invest in gold in Africa. His father had a great business sense. Richie knew it, and was never short of respect for his father.

He checked into the only hotel in Port Elizabeth: The Royal Hotel. To his astonishment, the owner of the hotel, a Miss Fitzgerald, was a close relative of his father. No one knew about her. He was amazed by this woman, who came from Ireland alone, survived the ravages of that time in South Africa, and was now the most influential woman in the town. He often asked himself if this was somehow meant to be, or if it was just a coincidence. He was never sure of the answer, but felt in his bones that fate had played a hand in their meeting.

The stories that Trudy Fitzgerald told him about growing up in Bruff, in County Limerick, had fascinated him. They spoke of a connectedness with a faraway land, which was something for which he longed. Something about Miss Fitzgerald's descriptions of his ancestral home had awakened something deep inside him that he did not know was there; something ingrained in the blood that ran through his veins. Thanks to her, he knew how people lived here on this land, worked, toiled and sweated to make a living. Miss Fitzgerald had described the house he now saw, and he had memorised her words about the laneway leading up to it.

In the distance a dog barked, perhaps aware of the presence of an outsider. Its ancestors, too, had quite possibly been here for a very long time indeed. Now he was here, but felt as though he were in a dream.

Richie was jolted out of his thoughts when one of the cows in the field next to him let out a loud bawl, causing him to jump. He reacted as if he feared for his life; as if he were about to be shot. It caused him to be nervous as he resumed his walk along the road, now totally in tune with his surroundings. Heartfelt emotions kept coming up as if from nowhere. He tried to ignore them, scarcely recognising them as his, but without any luck. Tears welled up from somewhere deep inside. He never felt like this about anything in his life before.

Pulling himself together and giving himself a little shake, he walked on. He glanced back at the cows in the field. 'Nice to meet you. There's no need to bawl at me.'

He did not know what to expect as his driver, Tom the hackney man, didn't know the family that lived here now. Or as Tom had put it, 'I know of them, but don't know them.' The family may not take kindly to strangers. Who knows how they would take his visit? Hopefully, they won't think he was there to claim back the land that once belonged to his forefathers. It had been in the Fitzgerald family name for hundreds of years.

It was said locally that once upon a time the house belonged to the Fitzgerald Earl of Glin, and the house had a history to it, which folklore had added to and taken from. Families had begun there and left there. It was still Richie Fitzgerald's ancestral home. Richie wanted nothing from the family that lived there now; he just wanted to meet the family and be in the same home that his father and grandfather came from.

3

His heart was beating loudly in his chest. He did not know quite what to expect. He felt as if he had gone back in time, but somehow everything was perfect in this moment. He knew, of course, that he stood out amongst the people here; the way he dressed and looked and sounded was different, and people he met made him very aware of this. Even so, his thoughts were happy thoughts. He knew about history, but that was hardly the same as being involved in the struggles that the people here had been through. They had suffered in ways that he had not, and had lived, loved and fought for their country. The fight for freedom had been long and cruel, and was rarely far from Irish minds. Much work was done by strong Irishmen, who worked silently and secretly behind British rule.

He knew from Miss Fitzgerald about the situation in Ireland, and how the struggle for freedom continued. Richie felt that he was in the right place at the right time.

2.

*B*ob's Mary had walked up this lane more than fifty years previously on many a Sunday afternoon, but with a very different attitude and agenda, with excitement in her heart, with a hop and a skip, and with devilment in her eye.

Mary got it into her head to seduce Dick Fitzgerald. At this, she failed. Dick was not interested in Mary's 'advances', no matter how she tried. Pulling her skirt over her head and baring all in front of him, which in her experience was sufficient to 'seduce' most men of her acquaintance, did not entice Dick Fitzgerald into her lair. And Bob's Mary was not lacking in experience. Dick Fitzgerald, however, was a good and noble man, and had no time for the likes of Bob's Mary, to her considerable annoyance.

Mary was a woman with enormous sexual appetites, and had a burning desire to conquer at every opportunity. In the face of resistance, which was rare enough, she would become obsessed, and would not stop trying. She enjoyed the thrill of the hunt. She loved the sexual act. She craved it. Sometimes her feelings and desires overpowered her. Her neighbours knew well that to conquer men was her main interest in life, as well as her biggest talent. Her accomplishments on that front were considerable.

I have him in the palm of my hand, she would reflect to herself with a wry smile. They won't be able to live without me. She chuckled at the thought. Many women much better than her would never know what she knew of their husbands. Once she knew she had them she would tantalise them by holding back from them. I'll make that fella wait, she would decide, like a cat playing with a mouse, and the hunger will be on him. He'll be desperate by the time he gets me. I'll teach him a lesson.

She had a following of sorts, known as the whistlers. That was the code: a long whistle followed by two short whistles. Mary would be seen leaving her home and coming down the hilly field to where there was a plateau. The grass was always flattened in the same spot. Men would come and go like clockwork. At times they almost bumped into one another. They all knew about each other's lovemaking with the bold Mary, but never spoke about it. They were ashamed and embarrassed to be linked with her. It was like an obsession. This was all the more remarkable because Bob's Mary was not attractive in any shape or form, except maybe for her long legs. She never wore any underwear. Winter or summer, it made no difference to Mary. She was brought up that way. Her mother had passed while she was a young girl. She had only her brothers and father. No one told her how to dress or keep herself washed.

Most women in the townland of Bruff hated Mary. A few, though, felt pity for her. Mary, of course, couldn't give a tinker's cuss whether they liked her or not. She would pass remarks to the women who slighted her. 'And where was your husband last night?' she would mutter snidely. These women would pretend they did not hear anything; mostly they did not want to deal with the problem that was Mary. They thought if they turned a blind eye or a deaf ear, no one would notice.

The situation was not one that should be underestimated. Ultimately, in Bruff at any rate, a woman's power over her husband came down to his sexual need for her. By withholding her favours on that front, a woman could 'persuade' her husband of almost anything. Mary's availability on that score, though, undermined the power relations in many a marriage. And Mary was nothing if not available. This undermined other women to the extent that Mary was treated as little more than a leper. One should never underestimate the attractiveness of availability. At Sunday Mass everyone wanted to sit as far away as possible from her, and that was before you considered her smell— a mixture of burning wood and stinking cows' milk. Not a regular washer, Mary would often refrain from washing until the morrow, by which time she would find that she was so busy during the day she would put off washing until yet another tomorrow. Often, tomorrow never came.

One thing was certain with Mary: she never forgot to apply the blood-red lipstick to her lips, and to a certain spot on her cheekbones, which she imagined gave her a healthy glow.

The likes of Bob's Mary will never be again. She was one of a kind. If Mary had kept a diary, or even been able to read and write, she would have some stories to tell and about God knows who. In the middle of the fields, and some would say the back of beyond, Mary lived a life that she only knew.

Her character was unusual. Yet she thought she was just the best looking the finest and the sexiest woman throughout the length and breadth of Ireland. She was in a world of her own, and she loved herself. Many a story was shared among the male community regarding what they had got up to with Mary. If it could be done, it could be done with Bob's Mary.

Her name, of course, was never mentioned by the men to their wives, which would be like a red rag to a bull. When Bob's Mary 'retired', beginning to suspect that she was not able for the younger men any longer, she had pains everywhere. But she couldn't help smiling that one snuggle-toothed smile when she was approached after Mass on Sunday mornings. She would seem interested in the proposition, but would let them down without ceremony. She would not make plans that she did not intend to keep. Even when she was long past her best, she would continue to hear the whistled code, by now from a new generation of Bruff's menfolk, and she could only wonder at what went through the men's minds, occasionally saying out loud to herself, 'Jaysus, they must be in a bad way. I'll keep them hanging on, so.' She would emerge from her front door, making shapes as if coming down the field, but then then turn in to the woods behind the house. You could see the biggest grin on her face. In her own view, hers was a life well lived.

Supply might have been wanting, but demand was as high as ever. In the absence of Bob's Mary, another woman who was well liked by the men of the countryside became increasingly in demand. She was always very discreet in her interactions with the local men. She had men who would call on her, never going out herself to proposition any man. There was no such thing as whistlers for her; she was entirely a more professional kind of woman. That said, she too loved the act of lovemaking, and to that extent was the successor of Bob's Mary. Her lovemaking prowess, it was said, was superior even to that of her predecessor.

Rural Ireland was a land unto itself, where the local inhabitants had a way of living and survival that only they knew. There was no real malice between neighbours, but when it came to land it was a different story. The land was handed down from father to son, continuing in the family name for generations. The sons of elders felt it a heavy burden at times, and lived in the knowledge that they would be considered a failure if they failed to retain every blade of grass for the next generation. It was their duty to fulfil the wishes of the forefathers: never abandon the land, and keep it in the best condition possible to be passed down to their own sons. One was less an owner than a custodian.

Practically none of the men made much money from working the farms; it was a case of living from day to day. As they lived deep in the countryside, their primary interest was in their neighbours, occasionally extending to the men or women who stood out in the local community, whom they would meet periodically over games of cards and dance nights in one of their homes, as well as on trips to the nearest town to stock up on supplies and maybe have a glass of porter while there. Milking farms would add to this routine with daily trips to the creamery. It would open at six in the morning, when farmers would already be lined up to offload the churns of milk. The day was scarcely long enough for all of the work that needed to be done.

Most men and women from the area were never outside Ireland, or as the locals would say, 'never a mile from a cow shit.' Even so, knowledge about the affairs of the world had a way of filtering into even the most remote corners. There were newspapers, there were stories. No group of people could have enjoyed the recounting of a story more, and so information and knowledge spread. Opinions were exchanged on everything from wars to the business of distant countries. Of course, their main source of conversational fodder was the matter of what was happening to Ireland under British rule, and whether Ireland would ever be free. A longing for freedom had taken hold, and was on many minds. Children would be sent out of rooms while adults gravely discussed 'the situation'. Many people who were motivated by little else still nurtured a conviction that they would do their part when the time came, whenever and whatever that was.

★ ★ ★

Biddy Bergin was a widow with no family of her own who lived about a mile off the main road. It was a winding lane full of overgrown ditches; grass had started to grow in the centre of the lane. She had been married for more than twenty years to John Bergin, a kind and good-natured man. Biddy was the outgoing one; she loved to chat and to have a laugh. John was always delighted when she would come home from town with all the news of the parish.

Biddy would say, 'John, do you remember that so and so, well that fella got his comeuppance over that ditch bounding the Burkes' and Dowling farm.'

Every inch of land, good or bad, was a most prized possession. John Bergin, like most farmers, loved the gossip and the happenings, good or bad, between them. He didn't have it in himself to confront anyone. He was a decent farmer, and got along with everyone. Many a neighbouring farm had issues with boundaries, or with farming families who shared the same laneways. There were always rows about rights of way, and about who was responsible for the upkeep of the shared lanes. Many an hour was spent spying on each other. When one family got a tractor it was like a revolution in the neighbourhood.

A dominant family, the Stauntons, owned the most land on the shared laneway. There were five Staunton brothers, none of whom was married. They took it into their heads to erect a gateway at the roadside of the lane, which was making it difficult for the other neighbours, who complained to the Stauntons and asked them to remove it. They were so hard-headed they wouldn't take it down, instead telling the other two families that the gate was staying, otherwise they would go to the law and have the police come down on them.

That night the Quirke family's four brothers and two sisters stayed up all night, and with a saw cut down the gate into twelve-inch lengths, and left it in the middle of the lane.

Stauntons, furious with Quirkes, saddled up the horses and went into Bruff and made a complaint to the police about the Quirke family. This was considered a terrible thing to do. A shameful thing to do.

The police duly came out to the scene of the sawn-up gate. The Stauntons were adamant that they would take the family to court so that they would be named, blamed and shamed.

The week before Christmas, the court in Bruff was sitting. When the case between the Stauntons and the Quirkes came before Judge Fitzpatrick, he was not happy with the goings-on between the families, who lived on the same laneway for years. He gave the Stauntons a right telling off: who did they think they were, erecting a gate without the consent of the other families who used the laneway? The Quirkes did not escape his wrath for taking the liberty of cutting the iron gate into foot-long pieces. He suggested they might have taken it down and left it to one side and not damaged it.

The courthouse was full that day, with many tinkers up for assault. The women were left outside because it was mostly the men who were brought up in front of the judge. If a woman was in the stand in front of the judge, she was considered a very bad person indeed. It didn't matter if she had been beaten by her husband; the man would plead that she was a no-good wife and mother, and the judge generally saw no reason to disagree, often giving the wife a warning to respect her husband and do his bidding, take care of her children and keep house.

Alcohol was the biggest thing among the tinker families. They drank to excess whenever they had money. In a recent fight in Bruff between tinker husband and wife, the woman could get no good from the man. She had a baby at her breast underneath her shawl. When her husband would not answer her, she threw the baby at him. The husband did well to catch the baby, at least this time.

The local newspaper, the *Journal*, reported on the court cases. Of the Stauntons versus the Quigleys case, Judge Fitzpatrick ruled that the conflict was to end, or that he would not hesitate to hand down custodial sentences. He remarked that there was no need for this kind of conflict, especially over Christmas. Throwing the case out, and refusing to award compensation to either party, he told the neighbours to get along with one another and find within themselves some Christmas spirit and goodwill.

John Bergin was at his happiest, or as he would have put it himself, 'in his glory.' Biddy relayed events of the day in court, what the courtroom was like, its wooden benches and its judge's chair. The respect and the ceremony of it all was something rare to see. It was a packed room with many men. When the judge entered, everyone stood, sitting again only after the judge sat down.

John Bergin took a keen interest in his neighbours' rows and interactions. He had many an opinion, most of which he shared with Biddy at the end of the day's work as they chatted, sitting by the fireside. John smoked the pipe, and would light up when they both sat down before going to bed.

The families on the laneway carried on as they did before, although nothing so serious as the cutting down of gates occurred again. They kept themselves out of court as they knew the judge would not look kindly on them if they returned, and it could have meant gaol for members of both families. As none of the Staunton family married (they thought there was no one good enough for them), the eldest brother, Timothy, was the boss. He was a stubborn man, hard to please, and his word was gospel.

Alas, John got very sick with stomach pains; he could hardly keep a bit of bread down. All he wanted to do was drink water, milk or tea. There was a deadly thirst on him. He longed for a cup of water from Lough Gurr, where he grew up. As a child he loved the water from the lake; it was cool and refreshing. 'Natural springs have the loveliest water,' he would say. 'If I could only have some of that water, I know it will take the thirst off me.'

When he went to the local doctor, the news was not good. Doctor Jim Walsh knew the signs of diabetes, which John had had for some years now. His kidneys were failing, and it was affecting his whole body. He gave John some medication, which he took diligently, but to no effect. He took to the bed, and didn't last long after that.

Biddy nursed him with loving care. 'It's only the two of us,' she would say, 'we have no one to depend on. We are better off this way.'

John would reply, 'I'm a burden on you, Biddy. I am not able to do a thing around here; you have to do it all.'

One night, the two of them had a chat about what would happen when he passed away, hoping that he would be better treated by another world than he had been in this one. Biddy said, 'You will go to your heavenly reward and wait there for me. When it's my time to go I will be longing to see you again. God will look after us; sure we never hurted anyone or stole anything or did anything wrong. It's only right that God himself will look after us. We are good living people. Although we were not blessed with children, sure we had one another. We wouldn't harm a fly.'

Biddy was able to reassure John that everything would go on the same as it did when he was out there helping her with the work. She would make sure that everything was attended to. She would employ help when she needed a hand.

With a little help from their neighbours, she felt that everything would carry on like normal.

Biddy had one cow, which she milked herself, and a few chickens for the eggs. She had a pony and trap for her visits into town. Shortly after the final chat, John duly passed away. All the neighbours for miles around came to the house to pay their respects to the man, who was looked kindly upon. The neighbouring women came to help her make the tea, and brought some cakes and bread to feed everyone who passed over the threshold.

After the funeral, everyone pitied Biddy, who looked lonesome. They offered help, some of them practically insisting that they would do some of the farm work for her.

As time went by, her home was getting very dilapidated, and needed a bit of whitewash. By now Biddy had other things on her mind. Biddy was too busy for any painting: with the men calling at night, and her trying to keep the work going during the day, she was tired. The locality named her the Merry Biddy.

She always had a smile on her face, and not a front tooth to be seen.

From time to time, she was known to hire a farm labourer from another part of Limerick. They didn't stay too long with her when they moved on again. It was too difficult to keep up with the entire workload and keep Biddy happy in bed also. She managed to keep going somehow.

In the dark of night, local men would make a visit to Biddy, none of them staying for long. The door was open at all times during darkness. She was not afraid of anyone or anything. When asked by the town shopkeeper how she was managing on her own, she laughed heartily and said, 'I am not afraid of anyone or anything. If I was I would be afraid of the living and not the dead.'

After many years passed, the lane became silent, except for the howling and screeching of foxes, badgers and birds. It was also the home to many rabbits, many of which ended up in stews accompanied by onions, carrots, parsnips, and some turnip when it was available. These stews would last a family for at least two or three days, being reinforced with dumplings made of flour. These would fortify many families against the cold.

The silence could be frightening. Children would roam freely through fields and woods, and would seldom meet with anybody else, for better or worse. Herds of cattle grazed in the fields as birds nested in the treetops. When the sun reached a certain point in the sky, children would return homewards, and pots of stew would be assembled.

3.

*S*eanie, a simple man with red hair and a long red beard, lived with his parents on the next farmhouse. They called him an idiot. He visited the local rambling house with the men, where they enticed him to call on 'Merry Biddy'. The smart lads, as they were called, put him up to calling on Biddy while they stayed hiding in the bushes behind the house. The devilment they got up to with poor Seanie was disgraceful. They were fit for anything. But there was no harm in them at all. They never really harmed anyone, at least not intentionally.

Seanie walked into the house, putting his hand over his willie, and asked Biddy to do the sexual act with him. He really didn't know what he was asking for. He pointed at his private parts and then put his hands on Biddy's private part. Biddy looked at him and asked, 'Do your mother and father know you are here with me?'

'No,' he replied, 'only my friends at the rambling house Byrne's.'

'Are they putting you up to this?'

'Ah, no,' he said, 'they want to make me happy is all.'

Biddy sat him down and tried explaining to Seanie that it was a trick; that they were only having him on and making an ass of him. 'Blaggarding,' she said. 'Making an eejit out of you while they are all laughing.'

Seanie didn't know what to do now. Confused and a bit scared, he ran out of the house down the long lane and home to his mother and father, where he told them what had happened.

Well, the family were livid with the local men. They went to the rambling house the next night and told off the men there. It did no good at all. Now they just tantalised Seanie more, telling him he was just a sissy and no-good eejit. Bob's Mary would, for the purposes of comparison, have told them to get fucked and mind their own fucking business. Biddy, though, was more reserved, was not as vivacious as Bob's Mary. She tried to be ladylike, and a bit above the neighbouring women. She never told anyone about her night callers. Privately, she scoffed at them, thinking to herself how amusing it was how little they knew about their own husbands. The men, in turn, never let it be known to anyone that they visited Biddy Bergin. While they got away with the visits, they thought there was no need to tell anyone where they were.

That is until one night, when Rita Sanders followed her husband, Peter, stumbling in the dark of night and trying to be as quiet as possible, knowing that her husband could turn around and see her at any time.

Peter walked on with determination, humming a tune that Rita never heard him hum before. They were only married six months, and Rita was hoping to get pregnant. Nothing was happening yet on that front, but her friends kept reassuring her that it would take time. 'Don't be in any hurry,' they said. 'Sure you'll have many babies all in good time. God is good.'

But she was uneasy about the whole thing. She wondered where her husband slipped off to three nights a week. He would say he wanted a break and was going to the Byrne rambling house to chat with the men there and maybe play a game of cards. He told her that women were not allowed to visit, that is until they had a house dance planned, when they were welcome to come and enjoy some tea and buns. Disappointed and lonely on her own, Rita was not convinced about the rambling house. That was when she decided to follow him.

She kept her distance, making sure she did not trip over any stones or briars. The moon was coming in, and out behind the clouds a cold night air was blowing. She noticed Peter checking behind him, standing and listening before he moved on again. He was not heading towards Byrne's rambling house; instead, he was heading down the fields towards Biddy Bergin's house.

As quick as a flash, he entered Biddy's kitchen.

Rita came close to the window, and could see Peter talking with Biddy. They were laughing and smiling at each other. She couldn't believe her eyes when the two of them headed down to her bedroom.

When peeping into the corner of the window, Rita could see what went on. Her heart sunk into her shoes. Silent tears and sweat flowed down her face. Somehow she plucked up the courage to stay and wait at the end of the lane to confront Peter.

She was only standing there a few moments when Peter came along, humming the same tune. She stood out in front of him. 'Jesus,' he said, 'where were you going this hour of the night? I was just returning home.'

'I followed you and saw what you are up to with Biddy Bergin. It's no wonder you are tired when we go to bed. It's not me you want at all; it's that bitch who just used you.'

'I married you. I love you.'

'Why?' she asked Peter. He would not answer.

She repeated her question. Peter Sanders just turned his back and walked away. Rita followed him, shouting and cursing him for betraying her.

'Everyone will be talking about us. You have brought shame on the two of us.'

'Ah, fuck off,' he replied. 'You are no good in bed anyway. I think I have married a nun.'

Screaming now, Rita replied, 'What do I have to do to keep you at home in our bed and stop going out to that bitch? I thought we wanted to start a family that's what you said anyway.'

'No,' he replied, 'it's you who wants children. I don't give a shit if we have them or not. I will keep going to Biddy; at least she knows how to please a man.'

At this point Rita did not know what to say or do.

She stood on the road in the dark of night. Her whole world had fallen down around her. The realisation of what was happening was just too awful. What was she to do? She waited for an hour or two, thinking he would come back to look for her. But he did not. When Rita pulled herself together and went home, Peter was asleep in bed. She felt unwanted, and decided she would sleep on the chair in the kitchen. Alas, sleep would not come. She walked into their bedroom and woke Peter, who was not a bit pleasant. In the end he said, 'Just get into bed and go to sleep. We will discuss this in the morning.'

Before daybreak, Peter woke and turned to Rita to make love to her. She lay there and just let him do his usual no-good lovemaking.

In the morning they both got up out of bed and began the day's work on the farm. Rita was not happy, but Peter went around with a smile on his face. 'You all right, woman?' he would say now and again.

'No,' Rita would reply.

'Ah, you will get over it in time.'

'I am going to kill that Birdie Bergin. Once she knows we are not long married she should not entertain you.'

'It's my choice,' he said. 'I will go to her whenever I want to, so you can get used to the fact that's the way it's going to be always. Biddy was always there for me whenever I wanted to have sex long before I met you. She was the first person I made passionate love to. She knows how I like to make love.'

'Why the fuck didn't you marry her instead of me?'

'You were recommended by the priest to my family. That's why I married you. Not because I love you or anything like that. I just have to put up with you now. Do your work here and keep me happy and all will be well. Besides, you might not need to kill Biddy Bergin—Sheila Rafter is about ready to do it.'

'What?'

'You should have seen the two of them fighting the other day. She was shouting at her, telling her she was going to kill her. She punched her in the face and knocked her to the ground, then jumped on top of her. It was something to see. "You shameless woman!" "Try taking care of your own husband why don't you and then I wouldn't fecking have to!" "I'll kill you, bitch!" It took four men to separate the two of them. And that wasn't the last of it. Sheila was threatening Biddy that she would get her in trouble with the British soldiers and Biddy called Sheila a British bitch.'

A few years went by. Both of them had the same routine every day. Nothing changed. Although Peter changed his mind about children. Many a neighbour asked him about having no children. Was he up for it or not? He wanted a family then, just to prove he was man enough to father children. Alas, it was not to be.

From then on, the marriage between Rita and Peter was under a lot of strain. Rita did not have any family, and Peter blamed her for not having any children. With the help of the parish priest and the support of Peter, Rita made contact with the mother and baby home in Limerick, she put in a request with the Sisters of Mercy. She asked for males as she was thinking they would need help on the land when she and Peter were getting old. The sisters of mercy were very accommodating. They had any documents to be signed at the ready. Included in the documents was a brown envelope with a request for a donation of £100. They wanted it paid every year until the boys were sixteen years old. They were not brothers, they came from different women. Beautiful little boys, who were loved dearly by Rita. She was so content with the two babies, life was good for her.

Soon the boys were walking and getting into all kinds of mischief, which Peter did not like at all. He could see that Rita was a real mother and loved the boys. He took it into his head he wanted a boy of his own. He asked for sex with Rita sometimes during the day, and every night too. It wasn't long before Rita became pregnant. Everyone was so delighted for her.

Soon they had a lovely baby girl, whom they named Sadie. Peter kept up with the sex, and the next year Rita had a son, who was named Peter after his father. Rita had four children in all, and with the two adoptees the family was now six.

Rita was the happiest she had ever been.

She had help around the house. Peter was more content, and didn't go to Biddy Bergin's house as often as he used to. He too liked doling out work for the boys.

All in all, it was a happy childhood for the Sanders children.

4.

*R*ichie jumped at sound of the dog barking. The dog came running for him, the fur standing up on the back of its neck as it snarled.

'Get off me. Get off me!' he shouted at the dog. He drew out a kick at the dog, but it kept coming for him.

Mrs O'Keeffe came running out of the door and called Brandy. 'Come here, you!' The dog turned around and went back into the house, its tail between its legs.

'Who are you?' Mrs O'Keeffe shouted.

Richie walked forward with his hand outstretched. 'I'm Richard Fitzgerald, but my friends call me Richie. My ancestors lived here once upon a time.'

'What ancestors are you talking about, sir?'

'The Fitzgeralds.'

'Oh,' she said, 'they owned this farm before we got it. I remember there was something about an old man living here like a recluse. Meant to have sat in his chair with a shotgun by his side. He rarely came out to the village, and when he did it was only for food. Was he your ancestor?'

'Yes, I'm positive this is the old homestead. I have done a lot of research. I met a Miss Fitzgerald, Trudy to her friends, who is a relative of mine. She lives in South Africa. She is an elderly woman with much knowledge of the business world in South Africa. Has the best recall of her youth growing up here in Bruff. Her childhood memories are very vivid. While we talked I imagined everything she told me about her young years; I lived those moments with her. I felt very welcome in her company, and felt like a child again listening to my own father's stories, handed down from his father. While she lived and loved Durban, often her thoughts were back in her homeland and with her family. It's her aging years probably taking her back. I'm sure I brought up some deep thoughts and memories for her. That old man was her father I'm sure of that.'

Mrs O'Keeffe looked him up and down, and was intrigued with his American accent.

'You don't sound like you have an African accent; it's more like an American one to me? Although I don't know what an African accent sounds like either.'

He explained that he was born and brought up in America, and went to South Africa to make investments in the gold mines there. At that time there was great excitement about the gold rush in South Africa, and many of his colleagues and friends were investing. He took it upon himself to go there and see first-hand how the gold was excavated from the ground and if the investment was sound and secure.

He was cautious about his investments, as most of the money was his father's.

Mrs O'Keeffe said, 'I know many young and old people who left Ireland for America to find work. But the ones I knew never came home again. They all like the good life over there and don't want to live like we do again. They all miss home, and especially their family. The men miss their mothers most of all. Most of them send money home to the parents, and they send the fare for their younger siblings. There is nothing for them here. Nothing except hardship, anyway. Will you come in and stay awhile?' She gestured towards the door.

The furniture looked old, and the house itself looked as if it needed a revamp. Yet Richie felt a sense of knowing how the house would be.

'I hope I am not intruding on you.'

'Not at all,' Bernadette, and her husband, Harry, said in unison. She continued, 'We love the company, and are interested in listening to your story, and we love the American accent.'

'Did you have company?' Richie asked. 'I thought I heard voices in the distance.'

'Ah, no,' she replied, 'it's just me and my husband. We have four children, one girl and three sons. The boys are out working on the farm, and my daughter, Aoife, helps me with the housework. She is a great cook. Come on in and we will chat.'

Richie walked behind Mrs O'Keeffe. She was of short stature with a head of black hair that was fixed in a bun at the nape of her neck. She had small, quizzical green eyes, and her face had a red complexion. She seemed to him to be a wily woman who knew what she was about. She wore a crossover apron that covered her from her head to below her knees. It was of dark navy with a little pink-and-blue flower on the fabric. This was the most common attire for farming wives.

'Don't mind the kitchen now,' she said to Richie. 'We have just had dinner and everywhere is untidy.'

As Richie stepped into the kitchen behind the woman of the house, he noticed that there was an awful lot of delph and crockery strewn around, and some plates of food left unfinished.

'I am sorry … maybe I came at a busy time for you and your family.' Richie nodded to Harry O'Keeffe, who was older by far than Bernadette. He held a commanding position at the head of the table. He wore a dark waist-coat with a pocket watch sitting in the chest pocket, and a white striped shirt with a button neck and no collar. He was unshaven, his hair combed back, with a big moustache under his nose. He looked like a strong and well-worn man.

'Not at all,' they both replied at once, for the second time. Harry nodded sagely from his position at the table. 'Sit down, young man. Pull up a chair,' his wife added. 'You will have a cup of tea, won't you, Richie?'

She went on to tell her husband, Harry, where Richie Fitzgerald came from and why he was there. Richie interrupted, 'Please call me Richie; that's what they call me back home.'

Bernadette O'Keeffe smiled and nodded. 'Richard, you're now Richie.' She removed the kettle from the hook over the fireplace and poured a strong mug of tea for him.

'I rarely drink tea; it's coffee most of the time.'

'Ah, well you won't get any coffee here, it's all tea!'

Bernadette put large slices of home-baked soda bread on a plate with some home-made butter. 'Get that inside ya,' she said. 'It'll do you good. It'll put hairs on your chest. If I had known you were coming I would have kept some dinner for you.'

Bernadette was making such a fuss. Harry said, 'Calm down, woman and let the man eat and drink his tea.' Harry was most interested in why he had come to Bruff. Richie explained again to Harry why he had come all the way from South Africa: it was an overpowering and over-whelming desire to come to Ireland and find out where his ancestors came from. He went on to explain how he met Miss Fitzgerald in her prestigious hotel in Durban, Natal. Richie explained he knew nothing of her until he checked into her hotel, and met her by accident in its foyer. It was something that was meant to be.

'Why on earth would I come to South Africa to invest and meet my relative? I was so overcome, listening to her stories, details of her upbringing and her keen sense of pride in her homeland. So impressed with Miss Fitzgerald and the country she came from. I wanted to experience the real Irish, the people and the land I came from. Since I set foot on Irish soil I feel a deep connection and a sense of coming home.'

Harry piped up. 'I hope you have plenty of money with you; times are hard here. A lot of us are starving. The British bastards are taking everything we have. Even the fish out of our waters they are shipping back to England to feed their own! They don't give a fuck about us. Some day ... some day ...' he repeated, and then fell silent.

Richie assured Harry and Bernadette that he wanted for nothing, he had enough money to stay for a while. He assured them that he did not want anything for nothing.

'Actually, I have a hackney man waiting for me at the road gate. His name is Tom.'

'Bernadette,' Harry said in a raised voice, 'go down to the road gate and bring that man up here and feed him.'

With that, Bernadette brushed down her clothes and out the door she went.

She found Tom standing talking to a neighbour. Bernadette called to him.

'Oh Jesus, missus,' he said. 'Sorry, I didn't hear you coming.'

'Hello, Jimmy,' Bernadette said to the neighbour. She asked Tom to accompany her back to the house for some tea and soda bread.

'Oh that's great, missus. Will it be all right with the yank?'

'I'm sure it will,' she said. 'He has had some bread and tea himself.'

'Isn't it a grand day?' Tom said, making small talk.

'How did you get the job of driving Richie Fitzgerald around?'

With a wry smile, Tom said, 'Well he called into the pub and asked for a driver! I'm the only one with a car; that's how it happened.'

'He seems like a nice kind of man,' Bernadette said. 'What you think?'

'He's a gentleman, Mrs O'Keeffe, that's what I think about him. He looks as if he is not short of a few bob.'

'All the women around here would love to meet him,' said Bernadette. 'He is so good-looking, and with that American accent they will all fall for him. Maybe he is a married man.'

'Don't know that, missus. Why don't you ask him straight?'

'Maybe I will,' she replied.

Harry O'Keeffe was in his element chatting with Richie Fitzgerald. He took his crooked pipe from the breast pocket of his waistcoat and gave it a few taps on the palm of his hand. He then produced a small knife and a square of tobacco. It was like a ritual: the cutting of the tobacco, the filling of the pipe, packing down the tobacco into the pipe. He then produced a long matchstick, which he stroked on the sole of his boot to set it alight. The resulting plume of smoke and the waft of the tobacco was very pleasing.

'Well, young man,' he said to Richie, 'what are you going to do around here?'

Pausing for a moment, Richie replied, 'Well, sir, I want to experience how my ancestors lived. I want to find out more about them. When I met Miss Fitzgerald she was so passionate about where she came from, and I became haunted by Ireland. My father is elderly and never stopped thinking and talking about his homeland. But it wasn't until I met Trudy Fitzgerald in South Africa that the feeling of wanting to come here took over. She encouraged me to come, and I made the journey. I wanted her to come with me, but she declined. She said that she was no spring chicken, although it was difficult to tell her age, she kept herself so well. Dressed in the latest fashion, and always had her hair to perfection. She was truly the queen of Natal. Her staff, the employees, she treated like family. They in turn adored her. She is the best business woman I have ever met. I am sure she has broken many a gentleman's heart. I would have loved her company on the voyage. I promised I would write to her once a week while I am here.'

'She sounds like quite a woman, so.'

'Quite a woman, yes.'

'And it must have been quite a voyage here, all the way from Africa?'

'When I left South Africa it was scorching hot, no rain for over a year. The soil was like dust. The Royal Hotel is near the ocean, and there was a sea breeze which raised the dust somewhat. The evenings got cooler; the hotel was open from the front to the back, and a gentle breeze went through from the back to the front. Huge fans were installed in the ceilings where someone worked swaying the fan forward and backward in the dining room. When I left they were expecting some rain huge clouds, which were blowing up from the sea. It was a blessing for the people to have rain fall on them. The voyage was rough and unsteady at times, I thought we would sink in the deep swell of the sea; the swell came over the boat and washed away one man who was on the mast! It happened so fast no one could do anything to stop him from going overboard. I was lucky to get a cabin on the first deck; the lower decks stank of sick. At least it was easy for me to get on deck. I had an old hand-drawn map that Miss Fitzgerald mapped out on her journey from Ireland.

'I didn't sleep a lot; often it was so unsteady that I was thrown out of my bunk on to the floor. I had the privilege of dinner with the captain and some fine brandy. He was a very hospitable man, who loved the company of his workers as well as the passengers on the ship. He told us many stories of how he had made it through the roughest of seas, how he managed to steer the ship for days on end, without any sleep. Yet he explained he would not work at anything else. He was fond of the sea, and especially *The Roisin dubh*. He owned it himself. He, like Miss Fitzgerald, was a good boss to his workers. But on the other hand he would take so nonsense. "Work hard and you will be rewarded," he would tell the men.

'Although many years have passed since Miss Fitzgerald made the voyage, the seas never changed: they are as rough as she told me. I knew more or less knew how it would be. It will take me a week to recover, although I do not feel any fatigue at the moment. It's exciting and overwhelming here in Ireland. It's a whole different world in comparison to Boston and Durban and South Africa.'

★ ★ ★

It wasn't long before Bernadette and Tom arrived in the door. Tom sat down at the table with the two men. Now Harry was driving smoke through the roof; the pipe was working well. Now and again Harry would remove the pipe from his mouth and talk, then back the pipe went again. Richie marvelled that it stayed alight, but somehow Harry seemed able to coax it back to life even after the longest of interruptions.

Bernadette was fussing around making the tea for Tom. 'Are you hungry, Tom?' she asked. 'Sure I am, mam, I haven't eaten since yesterday!'

'Oh, Jesus, you must be starving.'

Harry instructed her to cut some slices of the smoked bacon that was hanging from a crook over the fireplace. Bernadette put up a fine plate of bacon for both men. It tasted like nothing Richie had tasted before. He loved the smokiness of the meat and the salt. It was washed down, of course, by another mug of tea.

After about an hour or so chatting with their visitors, Bernadette gestured to Harry to go down to the parlour. 'What are we going to do about the men? Are you forgetting they are here in the house at all?'

'Well,' he said, 'these two men are not going to go to the British soldiers and squeal on us.'

'Are you sure, Harry? Maybe I will let them out through the dairy window.'

'Ah no, Bernadette. I'm sure they are honest men.'

Harry was a shrewd man. Like many a pipe smoker, he was not disposed to be in a hurry to do anything. He had sized up his visitors, of course, and had made the decision to put his faith in them.

Returning to the kitchen, Harry resumed his place at the table. 'We have company here in the house,' he said to Richie and Tom. 'Bernadette was feeding them when you called, Richie. They are fine men. They are on the run from the British soldiers, and we are keeping them for a few days until it is safe and they are ready to move on.'

Then the dairy door opened Bernadette and about ten young men entered the kitchen. Richie and Tom's mouths opened in amazement as Harry O'Keeffe introduced the Irish Brotherhood matter-of-factly to Richie and Tom. Tom, the hackney man, knew three of the men already: they were from his own locality. He had no problem with the Brotherhood; he supported the cause. Richie didn't know what to make of it all. All he knew about them was from having seen their meeting, briefly, in the back room of the pub on his first night in Ireland.

The men were quiet, and only spoke when they were spoken to. Gaelic was spoken between the men. Richie sat up in the chair. 'Is there anything I can do for you?'

Loud laughter from the men.

'I didn't mean to upset you.' Richie said.

The leader of the men, Eoin Burke, explained that if he could get the British out of Ireland that would be great. A wry smile from Richie.

'If I could do that, I would.'

Loud laughter again.

'If anyone could do it, it would be you, Richie Fitz,' chided Tom.

The men seemed somewhat on edge. Not trusting Richie, they seemed to be okay with Tom the hackney man.

After a few hours the whole kitchen was full of men, with Bernadette waiting on them all. Everyone was in good form. Harry O'Keeffe was telling yarns, with everyone listening and laughing. Richie, who had never seen anything like it, was enthralled. Many of the stories and anecdotes they shared concerned being on the run, ducking from house to house. He heard first hand about the struggle in Ireland.

Tom, the hackney man, joined in the conversation now and again.

In an instant, the kitchen door blasted open with what seemed to be a gust of wind. Wind came down the chimney, which blew fire and smoke from the grate. The men stood, jumping as if pricked by a pin, and were ready for flight in an instant.

'What the hell is going on out there?' Harry said to nobody in particular.

Bernadette walked out into the yard. Brandy the dog was shivering, and had the hair on his back was standing up. He was whimpering, but nothing was moved and there was no sign of anyone or anything. She petted the dog on the head and told him to lie down.

Back in she came. 'There's nothing there,' she said to the men. 'It was just a gust of wind. Although the dog was nervous too.'

'I never saw him nervous before,' Harry said.

'Nor I,' Bernadette agreed. 'It would give you chill running down your spine.' Even as she said it, a shiver came over her. 'Someone just walked over my grave.'

'What do you mean?' Richie asked.

'Ah, it's an old saying,' she said. 'It doesn't really mean anything; a little bit of a fright maybe. Whatever it was, it's gone now.'

They had experienced whirlwinds and small tornadoes before. Harry reminded Bernadette of last summer, when it rained hay from the sky.

'We went out early one morning, and I couldn't believe what I saw!' said Harry. 'The whole roof of the house was covered in hay: the yard, the sheds, everything! Everywhere was in darkness until it stopped when the sky finally cleared. I never saw anything like it before.'

Everyone in the kitchen had their own thoughts on the sudden wind, but not sharing with the group. Harry privately thought it to be more than just a gust of wind. He had felt the chill running up and down his spine. For him it was a reminder of stories he had heard as a young lad. He was so frightened of the Banshee—the immortal being who came to take the soul of the dying.

Certain families were followed by the banshee. Her screaming could be heard for miles. When she was heard, the neighbourhood knew she was coming for the soul of a neighbour. On hearing the screeching, everyone would bless themselves with the sign of the cross three times and say a prayer for whoever it was.

The bawl and screech of the Banshee was a chilling experience that would root you to the ground. You would be stuck to the spot with fear, and could only hope that it would stop.

Richie Fitz didn't think anything of the sudden wind at all, and did not understand what had happened or why the people in the house were concerned about it.

The atmosphere in the room changed. It got serious and somewhat silent. Any sudden movement, and the Brotherhood were ready for action. To get out of there with their life was paramount.

There was much work to be done before nightfall. Harry decided that he must go out and milk the cows, and he commanded Bernadette to fetch the buckets and join him in the milking parlour. Walking out the door, he called to the dog. 'Brandy, come on, chap,' he called. 'Clever dog.' Brandy, like his master, enjoyed his usual evening ritual. He set off like the wind down the lane.

Richie, Tom and the men remained in the kitchen under Bernadette's instructions. Tom tapped Richie on the arm and reminded him that it was getting late. What were they to do?

'We'll wait for the owners to come in from milking.'

The Brotherhood men stood and each one extended their hand in friendship to Richie, greeting him in Gaelic. '*Fáilte romhat, Dia duit. Dia is Muire duit.*'

Richie was very polite, accompanying each handshake with 'How Do You Do.' He enjoyed the lilt of the Gaelic language. 'I would love to learn this language,' he said amongst his how-do-you-do's.

After a while the couple came in with buckets of milk. Bernadette said that she would start churning for the butter. Harry took a mug, dipped it into the bucket and drank down the mug full. 'Ahh,' he said with approval, 'it's nice and warm.'

Standing in the middle of the kitchen floor, Harry suggested that Richie and Tom stay the night. It was, after all, getting late, and it could be dangerous to drive in the dark of night.

'We have a settle bed in the parlour, and you can lay your head down there, Richie. Tom, you can rest in the chair at the fire, or join the men out in the hay barn. That's settled now, lads,' he repeated. 'We'll rest now for the night.'

Richie and Tom agreed. 'I would sleep on a bag on nails,' said Richie. 'I am exhausted from the voyage from Africa. Sleep has caught up on me.'

With the full moon going in and out behind the clouds. A gentle breeze was blowing. Tom headed out with the Brotherhood in single file, watching and listening with every step they took. Not a sound was heard from the barn that night. Every man slept silently, laying down on a bed of hay or straw, which kept them warm for the night.

Richie headed to the parlour, but Bernadette stepped in front of him. 'Wait now,' she said, 'wait until I get some bed clothes for you. It gets cold down here at night.' She pulled at what was like a church seat with a back on it. When folded out it was a bed of sorts—a very hard bed of wood. A few blankets and a pillow from the drawer under the bed were pulled out. 'There are a few coats on the back of the door if you want more warmth,' she said. 'I hope they are not damp as they are there for years.'

'Hopefully I won't want them at all,' said Richie.

Richie looked around the room, he could smell damp or mould. The room was stuffy, and it seemed there was no fresh air coming in at all. He looked across towards the window at the back wall of the room. Its shutters were nailed shut.

5.

*I*t was a quiet night at the O'Keeffe's household. Bernadette and Harry headed upstairs to their room. Richie was stretched out on the makeshift bed in the parlour, jotting down a few notes in his diary. There was a complete silence of a kind that he had never known. Not a sound. Then, over in front of him and under the sideboard, he heard a scuttle and a squeak. He stopped writing and put down his notebook. He heard it again, but now it was coming from under his makeshift bed. This room, or 'parlour' as his hosts described it, was clearly full of mice, and he would be unable to sleep a wink.

He stood up and pulled out the bed. Sure enough, there were two small little mice. Startled, they ran under the floorboards. Richie put his shoe firmly into the hole in the floor with an air of finality, and it was quiet once again. Lying on his back with his hands behind his head, and looking up towards the ceiling, he drifted off into a deep and peaceful sleep.

Three or four hours had gone by when Richie felt a nudge in the arm. He thought it was someone coming in to wake him up. He sat up in the bed with the light of the moon coming in through the crack in window shutter. He could barely see around the room, but there was nothing there. He got up out of bed and walked around the room, checking if anything had moved his bag with his clothes and what cash, but everything appeared to be fine.

He didn't want to wake anyone during the night, and returned to bed. This time, though, sleep would not come. The clock seemed to click louder and louder. He closed his eyes and decided he would stay in the bed until dawn.

After a while he felt the nudge once again. This time he kept his eyes closed. He could feel someone's breath on his face. He opened one eye, but could see nothing there. This room is alive with ghosts, he reasoned with himself. I wonder do the O'Keeffes know about the goings on during the night? Maybe they put me down here to experience the ghosts of the past. Could it be that their ancestors were unhappy or uneasy?

Sitting upright now, he spoke aloud. 'Whoever you are I will not harm you. Come forward and speak to me. Let me know what it is you want, or want me to do?' He kept sitting up on the bed, waiting for an answer, Alas, nothing came, not a sound.

After a while he heard the O'Keeffes getting up out of bed and coming down the stairs. He was dying for a piss. He opened the door and called to Bernadette, 'Can you direct me to the bathroom?'

'Yes I can,' said Bernadette. 'Out the kitchen door there and into the long grass! No one will see you there. We won't mind you, anyway.'

Scratching his head at this, Richie resigned himself to taking a long piss in the long grass.

Walking back into the kitchen he caught a glimpse of Tom and the Brotherhood coming out of the barn. He waited at the door for them and greeted them with the biggest smile. 'Have you had a piss yet, lads?' he asked.

'Oh, we did long ago,' one of them replied, not making anything out of having to go in the long grass.

'What do you do if you have to shit?'

'The same thing!'

Richie thought this barbaric. No bathroom? How did they all survive here on this land? Were the women really happy to live in this way? He then remembered the O'Keeffes' sons and daughter—he had not seen them at all. Perhaps they were the ghosts of this other-worldly house.

★ ★ ★

Bernadette set about stocking the fire and filling the kettle over the crook. She had a basket of brown eggs on the dresser, which she cracked on the pan.

'This will take a while, lads,' she said.

'I will help you,' offed Richie.

'Not at all,' she replied. 'This is the woman's work. It's my pleasure to cook and feed you all.'

All day long Bernadette was busy doing chores and cooking. She never seemed to sit down, except to eat.

'How do you keep up with all the work?'

She laughed a hearty laugh. 'The day is not long enough for me! I am used to working. Sure I wouldn't know what to do with myself without it!'

Harry got his boots on, and beckoned at Tom, the Hackney man, to come with him.

'Bring two buckets, Tom, and I'll bring the others. We have a few goats that will need milking too.'

The dog, Brandy, was on hand to round up the cows.

'The goats could be anywhere,' Harry said. 'Maybe you and the dog will go down the lane? They are tied together, two by two. They could have gone as far as the road.'

When Harry had the three-legged stool under the cow, the men arrived at the milking-shed and asked to help.

'All right, lads. Pull up that other stool and put it under the black cow.'

Dennis Brown was used to milking. Harry had given him the quietest animal to milk. When the buckets were full, there was no sigh of Tom.

'The fecking goats must be gone to town it's taking Tom so long to bring them back!'

Harry walked to the door and whistled for the dog. After a few minutes, the goats, the dog and Tom came bombing it up the lane. The dog guided them into the hay shed, where Harry tied them to the posts. It was not that easy to milk the goats. Their horns were mature, and if you were not looking you would get a swift puck in the butt, or anywhere else you left open to attack.

Buckets in hand, the men returned to the kitchen, where Bernadette had the breakfast ready.

'You are some woman,' Richie commented.

'It's no bother, really. Sure I could feed the whole of Ireland. And I probably have!' She laughed. 'While I am able, and have the meat and eggs, I will do it with joy.'

Richie had worked up a hunger, and enjoyed the big breakfast.

'Jesus, a man would need to do hard labour for the day long after that breakfast.'

Quick to reply, Harry said, 'We can arrange that! We have to cut back the weeds and briars behind the barn today. The piggery will be for another day. Can you handle a scythe?'

'I can't say I've tried,' replied Richie. 'But I'll give it a go if you show me how it's done.'

'You will have blisters on your hands until they toughen up.'

The Brotherhood knew that they had to remain indoors during daylight, and only risked coming out while they were eating. Richie could see that it was not an easy life. Soldiers could arrive at any time and surprise them. The men knew they could be shot dead at any time, and without mercy.

The Brotherhood's operations were conducted under cover of night. With no moon to light the sky, it was possible to head out and check things, like where the British soldiers might be camped. Even that was dangerous as the British may have knowledge of the whereabouts of the men on the run. Worse, it was not impossible that there was an informer amongst them. Everything was possible, and these men were seldom able to relax. This took its toll, both physically and psychologically.

If the British discovered that the O'Keeffe house was a safe house for the Brotherhood, they would come and investigate, bringing death and destruction with them. Today, with the arrival of their new visitor, they would need to be especially on guard.

'Let's keep everything tight here,' Harry said. 'We take no chances today, men.'

The men returned to the barn.

'What about me?' said Tom.

'Sit down at the table and we will have a chat about that. You too, Richie.'

Bernadette joined the men at the table.

'Myself and herself were discussing this last night when we went to bed. We both agreed that you, Tom, should go back to your job in the town and make a living as you do. Richie Fitz, you stay here with us for as long as you want. You will need to help us out with the farm work because our children had to go to Bernadette's aunt and uncle's farm to help them out. Her husband, Mick, is sick. He had pneumonia; he is in the bed for the past week or so. The children were to return home last night. Things mustn't be too good there because they didn't return. Soldiers might have stopped them or came upon them on the way home. We don't know.

'Bernadette and I will need your help here. Would you rather stay here in the old home out in the countryside, or off in the town of Bruff?'

'That's great,' Richie said to Harry and Bernadette. 'I will do what I can to help you out. I am very happy to stay here and be with you all for a while. I already feel that you are like family to me.'

With scythes and billhooks, Harry and Richie headed out to the back of the piggery to start the work. Harry sharpened the tools on a stone before cutting a thing. He had to explain everything to Richie as he had never seen this kind of cutting before. He raised the billhook over his head, then brought it down low under the weeds in a smooth motion, with one swipe clearing away a whole row of briars and nettles. Every few minutes he would stop, take a breath and listen. Richie had the job of dragging the weeds away. His hands were getting stung with the nettles, and were bleeding from contact with the thorny briars. Harry stopped again, and told Richie to catch the nettles at the bottom of the stalk.

'You will only get too many stings. Get the power in your hands and get a good grip on them to begin with; they won't sting you then.'

That worked for Richie. It made him feel a sense of accomplishment, strength and pride at having mastered this task.

Before they had made much headway into the work, the dog began to bark, startling everyone in the house. The worry was of course the Brotherhood, and the possibility of the British soldiers finding them. That would mean woeful danger for everyone.

Harry walked to the side of the house with Richie behind him. He could see down the lane, but could not be seen where he was standing. He could see that someone was coming up the lane very slowly. When she got near, Harry shouted, 'Aoife?' She looked dishevelled, her hair blowing all over the place, her long skirt torn, her white blouse in tatters, and with no shoes on her feet.

Terror took over Harry. Bernadette was alerted too, and was out the door in a flash.

'Aoife!' she shouted, running towards her beautiful daughter.

Aoife collapsed into her mother's arms. Harry was holding on to both women, Richie looking on in a daze. The dog, Brandy, was over to Aoife and standing looking up at her.

The first words Aoife said were, 'Mammy, Daddy, I thought I would never see you again!'

Sobbing, the tears flowed down her face. Her father picked her up in his arms and took her straight to the kitchen and sat her down on his chair. Aoife could hardly speak; she was out of control with fear.

'Wait now,' he said to Aoife, 'Mammy will make a cup of tea for you.'

'No tea, Daddy, I just want to get sick.'

'What in the world happened to you? Where are your brothers?'

She began to tell what happened to her. 'The lads decided to stay on to help Auntie because Uncle was not getting any better. We all decided together that I would take the horse and return home. I was just about two miles from home, going past the Dillons' wood, when I think it was about six British soldiers came upon me. I stopped and dismounted the horse. They looked so angry at me. "Where did you get this horse?" they wanted to know. I explained it was not mine, that it was my aunt and uncle's horse. I only had a loan of it to come home. They didn't believe me, and started shouting at me that I stole the horse and would be killed dead because of it. That this was the law. They would tie me to a tree in the wood and shoot! I was so afraid of Dillons' wood and the spirits I nearly fainted.

'That wasn't the worst of it though. They tied me up all right.' Sobbing, she showed them the bruises on her wrists and ankles.

'They spat in my face, laughing and making little of me, saying things like "You think you are a fine woman, but you are nothing, only a whore." What does that mean, Mammy?'

Bernadette could hardly speak. Looking at her poor daughter, she dreaded what was going to come next.

'What did they do to you, child?' asked her mother.

'They pulled at my blouse. Look at it; it's in rags, and that was my good one. They mauled at my breasts; every one of them did that to me. Then they pulled down my skirt and knickers and did an awful thing to me. It hurt so much I could not even scream. Those men were making a mockery of me, Daddy; they treated me like an animal. They took out their big private part and shoved it into my private parts. While one of them was doing this the others were laughing and telling him to hurry up because they wanted their turn.

'When they had enough, they walked away and left me tied up to the tree. Auntie's horse was standing out in the middle of the field grazing. They removed the two bags I had from Auntie. She had some butter and cheese made for you. They took the lot. They took the horse.'

Harry gestured Bernadette to take Aoife to her bedroom—she may have been followed here.

Richie was shocked and angry at what had happened. He followed Harry out of the house while Bernadette prepared a bath of hot water for Aoife to clean herself.

'I will never get the smell of them off me, Mammy.'

'I am hoping to God they did not make you pregnant.'

Aoife shuddered at the thought of that. She was a virgin, and had never had any sexual experience with any man.

Bernadette knew that they had violated her daughter. It was the worst thing could happen to any woman on this earth. Those men had no morals or scruples. They were barbaric. 'There is no God in them,' she said to Aoife.

Aoife explained how after all night long shivering and so afraid of the spirits in the wood she must have fainted or passed out for some time. Maybe it was pure shock.

In breaking of the dawn she managed to get her hands free, then her feet. She ran as fast as she could, always glancing over her shoulder thinking the British soldiers would come out of nowhere.

When she got to the road gate, she almost collapsed.

Tears rolled down Bernadette's face as she put her hands over her mouth so as not to cry out loud and maybe upset Aoife even more than she already was. The thought of playing the situation down and telling Aoife it will be all right came first.

Richie was shocked. And for the first time in his life, he knew what it was to be truly angry.

6.

*H*arry O'Keeffe was on high alert out in the yard. The first thing he did was to go to the barn and warn the Brotherhood of danger of the British coming after Aoife and following her home.

There was no time to get organised. The dog barked viciously, warning that they were coming up the lane, rifles in hand.

Bernadette ran and locked the kitchen door. She shouted out to Harry in Gaelic to stay away from the kitchen. The Brotherhood was in severe danger of being caught. They had a plan made before this day, but now there was no time. They were here and were going to be caught, and that was it.

The leader of the men said, 'We will jump out the window into the piggery and out the opening in the wall.'

It was too late for Harry to tell them they were cutting the overgrown briars and nettles. One by one, they ran and jumped into the piggery and out the hole in the wall down onto the overgrowth. They lay flat on the ground under everything, holding their breath.

The soldiers entered the barn.

'Are you hiding anyone here?' the commanding offer shouted to Harry.

'No, sir, there is no one here. It's only me; my wife has gone to town. This man beside me is an American; his name is Richie Fitzgerald. He is over with us from Boston. His ancestors lived here many years ago. He has returned to see where they all came from. He just arrived here yesterday.'

'There is a motor vehicle on the road. Who owns that? Is it yours?'

They pointed to Richie.

'No, sir,' he replied to the soldiers. They were intrigued with his accent. He didn't know what to do, whether to shake hands or tell them to fuck off. He decided to remain a dummy and say nothing.

'Who is the driver of the car?' they asked.

'The driver, Tom, ran out of petrol yesterday,' said Harry. 'You may have met him on the road coming here; he had a can in his hand.'

'We saw no fucking man with a can,' he retorted.

Harry was doing his very best not to get angry with the men because he knew that would only make things worse then they already were. He wanted to kill the bastards, but knew that he must hold back now. He refused to allow visions of his daughter and how destroyed she was because of these hooligans enter his mind. He would not be helping her by getting killed. Gritting his teeth and clenching his fists without being noticed by the soldiers seemed to help.

Each soldier went around the barn, sticking their bayonets into the hay turf and any bags of firewood they had. When they were satisfied with that, they went to the piggery house. Looking out the hole in the wall, the men under the cover of the briars and nettles were not seen. They then walked out and round the back where the overgrowth was, with bayonets raised straight down into the weeds. When nothing happened, they walked away slowly out of the yard, threatening to return.

'Jesus,' Harry said, 'that was a close one.'

They found nothing that day anywhere on the O'Keeffes' farm. When the coast was clear, Harry gave the barrel in the yard a kick with as much force that he could. The Brotherhood understood the kicking of the barrel, and moved slowly out of the undergrowth.

'You must leave this house tonight and go on to your next safe house. Our family have suffered.'

'Ireland has suffered almost 800 years.'

'It's men like you who can free Ireland of the British. Reclaim our dignity and fight for freedom. We must look after our daughter, Aoife, and put all our energies into getting her well again.'

The Brotherhood was thankful for their stay with the O'Keeffes, and even more thankful that they had not been caught. It was a terrifying moment for the men. The situation had given the men renewed determination to fight for Ireland. Eoin spoke to Harry, and was very sympathetic with what happened to Aoife. 'We can only wish her the best and hope she will recover from this awful ordeal. The men that did this terrible act are monsters with no morals whatsoever. Bastards, that's what they are.'

'It was difficult for me to stay quiet while the British soldiers were here. I'm sure they are the same men who attacked Aoife. They think we are some kind of imbeciles who have no feelings and can withstand whatever they throw at us. It took all my strength to keep my mouth shut. If I'd have had my shotgun at my side things may have been much different now. Looking at the situation, it's just as well I didn't have the shotgun to hand. I would have blown them apart. Make them suffer and beg for mercy, which I'm sure Aoife did.'

'Do what you can for our country. Make Ireland a safe place to live in peace. I hope we will live to see the day Ireland will be free!'

The Brotherhood couldn't believe their luck. That night they moved on until daybreak.

★ ★ ★

Richie Fitzgerald was heartbroken for this family he had just met the day before. How could this possibly be happening? Thoughts were running through his head. What could he do for the family? For Aoife, especially. He did not interrupt the family as he sat at the table, and was filled with hatred for those soldiers.

Harry was in no mood to chat with anyone. He too was heartbroken for his only daughter.

Later that evening, Aoife seemed to have a fever. She was tossing around in the bed, her face red. She was sweating profusely. Bernadette spent every moment by her bedside. She prayed to the heavens above and every saint she knew of, pleading for Aoife's recovery. She kept a basin of cold water and some towels to hand to mop up the sweat and try and cool her down. Aoife was delirious.

As morning rose, Aoife went into a peaceful sleep.

Bernadette didn't know what to do for her beautiful daughter, and yet seemed proud that she withstood the rape and mauling of these men. How had she found her way home in the state she was in? It was a blessing really.

For three days, Bernadette never left her daughter's side. Sometimes she could see an improvement in Aoife, but then she slipped back into the fever once again. She talked little. Only when Bernadette insisted on a reply would she make an effort to open her eyes, and in a weak voice reply to her.

Bernadette started to worry even more when her daughter was unable to sit up in the bed. She was now unable to drink or eat anything. Harry and Bernadette decided to take their daughter to the hospital in Limerick.

Richie Fitz insisted that his hackney man, Tom, would drive his motor car and take them there. Richie knew that the situation was more serious than they first thought. Bernadette rolled her up in blankets while Harry carried her down the stairs and down the lane to the car.

They both went with their daughter to the hospital. Harry turned to Richie while Tom was cranking up the motor.

'Richie,' he said, 'I need a big favour from you. Now that you are here, look after the house and land until we get back, hopefully tonight. You will need help milking; we don't know when our sons will return home. Matt Henderson, one mile north, will give you a hand. He has a big farm himself, but is always willing to help a neighbour in need. Introduce yourself to him. They are a very good family.'

With the motor driving away in the distance, Richie headed north on the road. Many thoughts were flowing through his head. He was very concerned for the O'Keeffes' daughter, Aoife. He couldn't understand why those men raped that lovely girl. Her life would be changed forever. He had a feeling in his gut that she may not survive this awful tragedy. 'Hooligans!' he shouted out loud. What can I do to help Ireland? he thought, while standing to concentrate more. There had to be something he could do to help these people, this family, this country, this cause.

★ ★ ★

Matt Henderson was out in the fields when Richie called to the house. His elderly father was sitting outside the door on a stool with a stick in his hand. Richie explained that he needed any help he could get, and that the O'Keefe family's daughter was ill and gone to the hospital in Limerick with her parents. The old man was very sorry to hear the news, but informed Richie that his son, Matt, wouldn't be home before dark. He would give him the message, though, and said that knowing his son he would call over and help out with whatever he could. He also suggested to call on the Hennesseys over the crossroad: they had four fine, strapping sons. Hopefully they would be home today.

Richie bade farewell to the old man and headed down to the crossroads, unsure if it would be all right with Harry. However, he also knew that the cows and goats would need milking, and that he was ill equipped to do it without assistance.

When he reached Hennessey's he got lucky: the boys were out in the yard in front of the house. With the biggest American accent, he bid them good day.

'I am Richie Fitzgerald. I come from Boston, USA. I am at the Fitzgeralds' … oh, sorry, the O'Keeffes' home.' He explained about their daughter Aoife's illness and that she had gone to hospital. He needed help badly with the animals.

'Not a problem,' they said, 'we will come over with you now and be back for our own milking.'

Richie was relieved that he had the company of the four young men and that the animals would get milked. The young men stayed on until late evening, and got all the yard work and the milking finished. Richie was so very grateful to these young men. He didn't know how to thank them enough.

When they were leaving the O'Keeffes' home, they asked Richie, 'What are you doing tonight?'

'I will be staying here in the home, looking after everything for the family.'

'Tomorrow night, would you be interested in coming to the local gathering house? There will be a session there, some music and yarns told.'

'I will have to wait until the family return home before I can come to your gathering house.'

'Just remember to come to the crossroads: it's the third farmhouse on the left.'

'That I will do soon, hopefully,' he replied.

Richie was hoping that the family would return that night. When darkness fell he knew that he would be alone in the house. He decided to sleep in the armchair beside the fire, stoking the fire and bringing in more wood and coal, boiling the kettle on the crook over the fire to make himself a nice cup of tea. He also had some soda bread. Stretching out on the chair, he didn't feel comfortable. He needed something to cover him and stay warm. He went to the parlour. Instead of blankets off his bed, he took the old coats hanging from behind the door, settling down again and drawing the coats up to his neck and fixing them around his legs. He fell asleep.

Suddenly, he awoke, something moving around his neck. Whatever it was it was tightening all the time. What the hell could it be? A coat?

Loosening the neck of the coat with some difficulty, he moved it lower down on his chest, and returned to sleep. The coat was constricting like a snake around his abdomen. He awoke, gasping for breath.

'Man,' he said out loud, 'what's wrong with this old coat? It's having a life of its own. How could that be?' Something very scary was happening.

He decided not to sleep any more that night. He went over to the kitchen table and sat down with his arms on the table and his head resting on his arms. He was watching for any movement from the old coats.

The fire lit up as if he had stoked it, flames running up the chimney. The chair opposite him pulled back from the table. The hair stood on the back of his neck.

Brandy the dog was howling and squealing as if he had been hit with some object. 'This place is gone mad.' The life was frightened out of Richie Fitz. He couldn't stand it any more. He stood and walked to the kitchen door. Putting his finger into the holy water font, he blessed himself three times. He looked back at the fire, which was almost quenched. 'Weird things are happening here.'

He walked out into the yard; everything was so still, and darkness was all around him. Sitting on the stool that was beside the kitchen door, he decided to spend the rest of the night sitting there.

It was not long before daybreak, and he was never so glad to see the sun come up behind the hills in the distance. A ray of light was a ray of hope for him. A hope that whatever spirits were around during darkness would not be there during the day. He felt very anxious and tormented. He was listening for any sound, when the cock crowed he jumped off the stool.

Whoever passed or died there must not have had peace yet, he reflected. When the O'Keeffes returned home, hopefully today, he would discuss the happenings during the night. He was not going to spend another night alone in this house. Richie had never experienced anything like this ever before, although Miss Fitzgerald had shared the old stories of the past about the Banshee. Bob's Mary had shared stories with Trudy too frighten the living daylights out of her, which she in turn shared with Richie.

What if he had evoked some spirit with him staying in the house? Was it because he was a young man coming from another country? Before he came to the O'Keeffes' home, he did not believe in any of those stories: they made him laugh, and he was quick to dismiss them. Not now. He was frightened, and could not understand what was happening. Whatever it was, he did not want to experience a night like he did.

7.

*W*alking down the lane towards the road, Richie heard the car coming in the distance. Not a lot of cars passed along this particular road, and he was confident that his hosts were returning.

He waited at the road gate. The car came and stopped. Tom, the driver, Bernadette and Harry got out with a very sad look in their eyes.

'Aoife?' Richie said to Bernadette and Harry.

'She will remain in hospital for a while; she has not recovered from the savage brutal rape by those men.'

Tears running down Bernadette's face, she spoke in a low voice. 'God is good; hopefully she will make it home to us. She is in good hands in the loving care of the nursing sisters and doctors.'

Tom said nothing. He too had a sad face on him.

Harry enquired about the milking and how Richie had got on with that. Richie let Harry know that everything was taken care of and that there was no need to worry.

'I will get the horse and cart ready and go to the creamery with the churns of milk.'

'I will come with you,' Richie said.

'Right,' Harry said, 'come on then. We have to hurry, otherwise every farmer will be there in front of us.'

This was the time while jogging along in the horse and cart to get Harrys ears listening. About a mile down the road with not much conversation, the two men jogged along. Richie was holding back to wait for the right moment. It did not come. In a round-about way, Richie began the conversation about spirits and ghosts.

'Do people believe in these happenings?' he enquired of Harry.

That got Harrys attention all right. He looked over at Richie, a blank look on his face.

'Do you believe there are spirits?'

Richie explained hearing the stories from Miss Fitzgerald in South Africa. He did not take it seriously then, but now he was not so sure. He explained to Harry what had happened the night before.

'Ah, your mind was playing tricks on you. It's because you were alone in the house. It got the better of you is all.'

'No way,' Richie said. 'I heard what I heard and saw what I saw.'

'We will stay up until dawn tonight and see what will happen.'

Everything was going around in his head. Richie doubted himself and questioned his sanity. But he could only conclude that what he heard and felt was real.

The day's work began with taking the churns of milk to the creamery. They were just coming down the hill to the creamery when they pulled up to join the queue. 'Ah Jesus, we will be here all day.'

Getting down off the cart, Harry introduced Richie to the local farming community. Everyone wanted to listen to Richie he was like a celebrity. What was it like living in America? Were there many Irish people there? What was Boston like? Richie was very forthcoming with the details, answering the questions as best he could. Time went by quickly with all the chatting going on.

On the way home, driving the horse along the road, Richie chatted with Harry of his concern for Aoife.

'It was so cruel. That young woman had a good life before her, and now she is destroyed by those men.'

He wondered if she would ever come right again. He was so sad for Bernadette. How would she cope with this awful situation?

Harry, too, was all out of sorts. He was not the same man he met on the first day he arrived here in his old ancestral home.

When Richie and Tom the Hackney man were alone, Richie asked him to walk down to the road gate with him.

'What do you think about Aoife?' Richie asked.

Tom replied, 'It's serious: the nursing sisters have her isolated in a ward on her own. She seems to be sleeping heavily all the time. They said she is not in a coma and that they have sedated her to help with the recovery. The sister in charge said this was the best way to deal with this kind of shock. She assured the O'Keeffes that everything possible will be done to assist her recovery, but that it will take time for that to happen. 'It will be a wait and see now, Richie,' he said. 'I am not sure if she will ever recover though.'

Richie felt a fire in his belly. Anger started to rise up in him.

'How could any man do that to a young woman who never harmed anyone?'

'Richie, this is happening all the time here, and in other parts of Ireland too. The men and soldiers from Britain don't care about us. They treat us like scum of the earth. Its no wonder the Brotherhood are growing in numbers. They will soon be ready to free Ireland.'

'Do you really believe that will happen? I have only seen some men in the pub the first night I arrived here and again at the O'Keeffes' home.'

'That's just a small amount you have seen, Richie. Men are leaving their homes, wives and children to join the Brotherhood. As each day goes by more men are joining in the struggle to free Ireland.'

'What about you, Tom?'

'I do my bit too. I use my motor to help out the men any way I can. It is not easy with the motor as the British soldiers are alert to this kind of travel or moving men around. I have been stopped by them many times in the past, thrown out of my motor and left on the side of the road while they ransacked it. I am lucky they did not take it from me.'

The two men spent an hour or more at the road gate.

Walking back up the lane, Tom turned to Riche. 'Do you want me to stick around here and wait for you, or do you want me to move on?'

'Wait for a week. I will have time to consider what I am going to do. I have another situation to deal with as well.'

He told Tom about the happenings during the night. Tom, however, was not surprised, and seemed to take these things in his stride.

'These kinds of things go on in some homes through Ireland. Folklore has it that they are spirits that are not passed over. That they are trapped in a kind of no-man's land, stuck between heaven and earth. Most people who pass over do so without anything like this happening; they need to be freed and allowed to go to their heavenly reward. Mostly they do not harm anyone. A Mass needs to be said in the house to free those ghosts.'

'God, I couldn't suggest a Mass at this time; the O'Keeffes have enough to worry them. Do they already know what is going on in the house during the night?'

'They might or may not,' Tom replied.

'If they know, they have learned to live with the spirits. But maybe they don't really know.'

'Now is not the time, anyway,' said Tom.

Before they entered the kitchen, the two men decided that they would help out with the yard and milking work, hopefully making things a bit easier for the O'Keeffes. Tom offered Harry his motor car any time he might need it.

'I will take you up on that,' Harry said. 'Bernadette will need you to drive her to St John's hospital in Limerick in a week's time.'

'It's a blessing that you are here with your motor.'

'No bother, sir,' replied Tom.

Richie asked how he could be of help, and what were the most pressing things that needed to be done.

'Every pair of hands will help us a lot,' Harry said, his head bent down, looking at the floor.

Bernadette was working away silently, baking bread over the fire, another pot hanging from the crook over the fire with a lovely waft of stew permeating through the house. As soon as the bread was ready they would sit down and have some breakfast.

The day went well and all the work got done.

Nightfall came, and Richie asked Harry about the rambling house that the young men had told him about.

Harry knew the home well. 'The Byrnes are a welcoming family who enjoy the company of others. I spent many a night there as a young man looking for the right woman, and I found her—she is cooking for us here now! They would fix you up with a woman too,' he said with a smile.

Tom decided that he would accompany Richie to the rambling house. Tom was excited to visit this house with Richie. Everyone would want to hear him talking with the American accent, and the women would only fall for him. With the directions from the Hennessy boys, they set off.

★ ★ ★

After about a mile or so, they saw light coming from house set in off the road. The sound of a dog barking alerted the household to strangers coming. 'Shish,' Mick Byrne called out.

Knocking at the door. A male voice shouted, 'Come in, the door is open.'

In walked the two men. There was a crowd of people sitting at the kitchen table playing cards. On the middle of the table a candle was giving them light. A plume of smoke and a waft of tobacco filled the room. Everyone in the kitchen stopped and looked at the unknown men.

Tom was the first to introduce them. Their mouths opened when they heard Richie. 'Sit down, men, over here by the fire. Make way for the strangers,' a man with a long white beard said.

The two men sat. Everyone was interested in the strangers. 'Who are you?' the bearded man enquired.

Richie spoke, and explained why he was here. Tom too told them of his motor car and how he was driving Richie around. As the night progressed, the stories got scarier, the laughs louder, and shrieks could be heard.

When it was almost daybreak the crowd of men dispersed. Just before they left, Mick Byrne announced that there would be a dance in the house the next week. 'Youse are to spread the word so as the ladies will hear and come, otherwise it will be useless. We need the women to warm the cockles of our hearts. Musicians and step dancers too. The women will make some sandwiches, and we will have a drop of the poteen as well.'

Richie was enthralled with the way things were organised, all of it accomplished by word of mouth. Excitement went through the men as they walked back to their homes. Richie and Tom agreed to return the next week for the hooley.

While waking back to the O'Keeffes', the sun came up on a new day. 'I won't need any sleep,' said Richie, 'I am done sleeping here.'

As soon as they entered the house, Harry and Bernadette came down the stairs. 'Good morning, men,' they both said together. Off out to do the jobs Harry went, with Tom following him to the cattle shed. Richie stayed chatting to Bernadette while she was stoking up the fire and making the breakfast, sharing how the Byrnes welcomed them into their home, filled with the crowd of local men. The stories they told just rolled off Bernadette like a duck.

'A lot of those stories are just made up, you know that?' she said to Richie. 'It's like it grows and gets longer and scarier as it is handed down from generation to generation.'

'Jesus, I was really taken by the stories ... at times the life was frightened out of me! Do you believe in ghosts?' he asked Bernadette.

'Not at all,' she replied, 'there is no such thing.'

'Are you sure?'

'Well as long as I am here I have neither seen nor heard one. But we have heard stories about this house before our time here. There was supposed to be a ghost here sitting by the fire, much like the old man Fitzgerald. Dick, I believe his name was. Some people said that they even saw him sitting with a shotgun by his side, long after he passed away. Anyway, when we acquired the land and house we had a Mass here to put at rest any ghosts or spirits that were here. Sure it can't hurt, can it?'

Richie wanted to tell her about his experience the night before. He had to hold back because now he was thinking he may have dreamt it all. He was unsure of himself. But he made the decision to leave the house and move into Bruff.

'I will be moving back into Bruff,' he told Bernadette. She immediately said she wouldn't hear of it. He was to stay as long as he wanted to, as was Tom. They liked the company, and the help with the milking. With their sons away and Aoife in hospital, they were under pressure.

Richie suggested that Tom would take them to Limerick hospital today or tomorrow. Bernadette jumped at the chance, saying that they would go later today. 'When Harry comes in after milking we will arrange a time.'

Richie decided that he would go with them and stop off in Bruff on the way. He wanted to buy some warm clothes and some boots. It was arranged to set off at twelve noon.

Tom hurried to get the motor ready. They headed out down the lane to the engine running on Tom's Hackney car. The journey into Limerick took about an hour or so. Driving along, the poverty of the people they passed along the road was evident. 'Those people have nothing,' Harry remarked. 'They were comfortable and wealthy enough. They lost everything to the British. They just walked out the door of their homes never to return. They wander the roads and beg food from the local farmers. It's no way to live or bring up children. When it rains or snows they bed down under any big tree. I don't know how they survive at all.'

Richie felt sadness in his heart for those poor people.

At the hospital, Harry and Bernadette went to the ward where they believed their daughter to be, but she was not there; she had been transferred to the second floor where the psychiatric patients were housed. The sister in change of the ward said that they would have to wait a while until they were ready to let them into the ward.

Harry and Bernadette sat outside in the corridor; they could hear screaming, shouting and crying. They could only imagine what was happening to Aoife. After a long wait, they were called in and ushered to the end of the ward, where Aoife lay in bed with her eyes closed, her mouth opened. They sat at either side of the bed. 'Aoife, wake up. Aoife, wake up!' Bernadette kept repeating, while Harry just stared and said nothing. Bernadette stared to cry and could not stop. Their daughter was not long for this world, Harry thought.

'We will take her home with us,' said Bernadette.

'I don't know if that will do any good for her at all. Maybe she needs more time here with medication,' Harry said.

After spending two hours sitting and waiting for her to wake up, they decided to have a chat with the nursing sister. When they asked for her they were brought into a room beside the ward, where they were seated in front of a big wooden desk with a green leather top. Folders and papers were everywhere.

There was a huge big window from floor to ceiling behind the desk, which the sun came through so brightly it lit up the room, which smelled of methylated spirits. With the brightness of the sun it was difficult to make out the details of the stern-looking overweight sister who sat behind the desk. Before they could ask a question, the sister said, 'You can see how your daughter is … there is nothing we can do for her. We're just keeping her as comfortable as we can. It would be a miracle if she got better.'

The sister explained that their daughter was in a coma-like state, possibly brought on by sheer terror and extreme shock. 'What happened to her … she may never get over it.'

'What can we do to help her?' Harry asked.

'Nothing,' replied the sister. 'We will do what we can with the limited nursing skills we have here in this hospital.'

'Could she not be moved to a calmer ward?' asked Bernadette. 'Or even to another hospital, or a nursing home near Bruff. The noise in here is just ... I mean ... it can't help. The noise of the other patients might be upsetting her.'

'Not at all,' the sister said, 'she does not know what is going on around her.'

Bernadette and Harry were shocked at the words the sister said. Her final words were: 'It will take a pure miracle for recovery.'

What they saw that day in the hospital ward would remain in their hearts and minds for the rest of their lives.

8.

With heavy hearts, the O'Keeffes left St John's Hospital, Limerick. Tom, the hackney man, was sitting in his motor outside the hospital. He did not ask how Aoife was because he could see on the O'Keeffes' faces the anguish they were going though.

'We will get something to eat before we hit the road home. Where can we find an eating house here?' he asked Tom.

'We will stop at Brennan's; it's about half a mile from here.'

Bernadette did not speak. She looked stunned. Her only daughter, whom she loved dearly, was not the girl she met today. Harry did his best to keep some conversation going, small talk about the weather and the surrounding lands they were passing along. Bernadette had only one thing on her mind, and that was a miracle for Aoife. It must happen, she vowed to herself. We must make it happen. A Roman Catholic devoted to prayers and novenas, she began to form a plan in her mind. She would begin fasting, going to Mass every morning of the week, and of course Sundays too. She would offer up her fasting and prayers for the return to good health for her daughter. She decided to involve as many neighbours and friends in her quest for a miracle as she could. She would get a petition going. All the prayers could only help Aoife, and she would tell the neighbours so. And so a vigil was begun, where at all times, day and night, someone was praying for a miracle....

★ ★ ★

Someone in the surrounding area heard about the bleeding statues in Templemore, County Tipperary. With the news of these miracles, many neighbours and friends accompanied Bernadette to Templemore, where they joined a huge crowd of people from all corners of Ireland. Harry O'Keeffe was not nearly so convinced that the power of prayer would do a lot to aid Aoife's recovery. But her mother did. She had strong faith and believed fervently in prayer.

Meanwhile, their two sons, John and Brendan, had returned from helping out on the relative's farm. Shocked and stunned, they took Aoife's rape and torture very badly. The two young men lost all colour in their face. Their pain was noticeable. They joined in the vigil and prayers for Aoife. A black cloud was over the O'Keeffes' farmhouse.

★ ★ ★

Richie Fitzgerald had remained on in Bruff, staying in its only hotel: O'Sullivan's on the main street. He kept in touch with the O'Keeffes. Once a week he had Tom drive him out to the O'Keeffes' home. He also checked the hospital in Limerick, and brought details of Aoife's condition. The O'Keeffes had given him permission and the authority to get an update from the nursing sisters.

He was flabbergasted to see how Aoife was treated at the hospital. As far as he could see there was not much the hospital could do for her except keep her sedated and somewhat comfortable. He felt that her surroundings were not helpful at all. He thought of the hospital back in Boston, and wondered if perhaps a psychiatrist should come to Ireland to see Aoife.

He was mindful of how the O'Keeffes might take his suggestion as he knew that they were a private family and would not want anyone except the immediate family to know what had happened. Nevertheless, he was going to put it to them on his next visit. The hospital would have to agree to allow this physiatrist to treat Aoife in the hospital, but it was the only thing he could think of that may help.

Richie became well known around Bruff and Limerick. He had put an order in to Ford motor cars for the latest model to be delivered to him: a T3, which was being built in Cork. The Cork Ford factory was very busy. Anyone who had money was getting in to driving a motor car. It was becoming a status symbol. The ordinary folk that did not have such a thing were looking up to the people who owned one.

Richie had placed a special order for leather seats and a black top and red bottom on the motor. He wanted to stand out in the community and be well known and well liked. back in Boston, he had a Cadillac from General Motors, which was the car of choice for the wealthy inhabitants of those parts.

Richie had a long conversation with the O'Keeffes regarding the doctor. The O'Keeffe family disagreed with bringing in a doctor from the United States. They thought that would be just impossible. It would take many months to organise this, and even then it would probably do nothing to help their daughter. With this conversation, Richie knew that they wer beginning to give up on Aoife. Or give up on reason. A miracle was what they wanted.

He explained to the family the advances in medicine in the USA. He had hoped that this intervention might work, but still they declined the doctor. Bernadette believed in the power of prayer, and kept all the novenas going with the help of her neighbours. 'We will leave it in God's hands,' she said, and the family agreed.

Richie was well known and well liked by the people of Bruff and surrounding area. The ladies of the locality fell for him, many attempting to conquer Richie's heart. As Richie walked around the town in early morning, many a poor soul approached him. It was mostly homeless women from the tinker community, often with an infant baby underneath their plaid shawl. 'Money for milk for the babba, sir?' This they repeated, over and over, again and again. To Richie, they looked as if they needed a good wash. Their hair was often stuck to their heads, muck on their faces, and sometimes blood streaming down.

One afternoon while Richie was out walking he noticed a tinker couple in the doorway of a shop. They were arguing. The woman wanted money from her husband for drink. He shouted, 'No, no, no!' With that she took the baby from her breast and threw the baby towards him. He managed to catch it before it hit the ground. Richie was shocked, but he remained silent. He knew better than to intervene between man and woman. His thoughts were for the baby, God help it. What would happen to it? What chance did it have in this family? Not a lot. How could anyone do something so dangerous?

He walked on, down by the Morning Star River, which flowed down through Bruff. At the end of the town there was a bridge, which was used by all in Bruff. The walk beside the river was heavenly, especially in springtime.

Two ladies in particular make it known that they wanted to marry Richie. They had to stand in line though. The yank had brought the town of Bruff to life. Every move he made, down to the details of what he had for breakfast, was uppermost in the conversation of the local ladies.

Richie had decided to go to the Byrnes' social night, and asked Tom to accompany him. Tom was becoming fond of Richie, and loved the attention they were getting, especially from the ladies, even though Tom had a wife and family, he was noticeably attracted to the ladies. When Richie would remind Tom of the latter's marital status, he would joke, 'Sure, but who could resist? You bring the women to life around here. You are like a celebrity. Jaysus, you are like a king! They all want to talk to you and feed you. No one ever noticed me like that before. Now that I am with you it's all different. They love you, and I am only basking in the reflected glory, so I am. It's great altogether.'

On the night of the Byrnes' house party, Richie noticed this woman, or girl. It was hard to guess her age. She was standing with her back to the wall and not taking much notice of him at all, unlike most of the other women, who were falling over him with their chatter and their invitations to more social evenings. People came from miles around as word of these social gatherings seemed to spread like a disease. They were particularly well attended by the young, free and single.

The night began with Rita Byrne and her two daughters sitting down the guests as they arrived for tea, bread and fruit cake. When each one was finished another took the seat at the table in the parlour. They kept feeding everyone that came up until midnight. The chairs and tables had been moved out of the kitchen to make room for the dancers. Then the dancing got going strong. During a break in the music, someone would be asked to sing. Most old Irish songs had about thirty-two verses, which afforded the musicians a sufficient break. If someone was out of key, it could be painful. Nevertheless, they listened to the song till the end. The person responsible would not be asked to sing again, regardless of how enthusiastically they volunteered.

Many of the men and women were known to be good dancers. They got asked out to dance the most. Some girls and women were a bit shy, but once they got out dancing the shyness abated.

Richie was somewhat awkward in this company. He did not have the first clue how to dance, nor how to do a 'Siege of Ennis'—a particularly popular dance, to which everybody but he seemed to know the steps. Even so, he did his best to join in, and there was no shortage of ladies willing to show him the steps. After a while, he began to feel light-headed with all the spinning around and dancing. He had never seen anything like it before, although his father often talked about Irish dancing. He made his excuses and departed from the dancing, making his way outside to have a piss.

'They have some energy in this house, Tom. How do they keep going?'

'They work hard is all. People who work hard relish a dance or two, and a social evening. Sure, there's nothing like it so. Those are some bloody good musicians in there; it's bound to get your feet tapping! Annie Murphy will come on the floor soon; she is a brilliant step dancer. Just watch her doing the Jig.'

'I saw her there coming in as we came out here.'

'Do you fancy any of the women?'

'The one standing with her back to the wall. She has a lovely face and beautiful long black hair. She is wearing an olive green skirt and blouse. Who is she, Tom?'

'I'll find out for you.'

'Don't make it too obvious, Tom. For all I know she might be missing some teeth or something!'

'Most of the people here come from a farming background, and are well established. Any single women here would be a good catch.'

'I didn't say I wanted to marry them,' Richie said. 'But I wouldn't mind kissing that girl.'

'Sure, ask her to dance why don't you? What's the worst that can happen?'

'I cannot dance very well. Everybody knows the steps but me. Not all of us were born knowing how to do it.'

'You can try anyway. You won't be made a show of here; everyone knows you have come from America and will have to learn the steps. What about a waltz?'

'Yes, that's probably better. Do you know this girl's name? Maybe she is too shy; she is not talking to anyone, just watching everything going on.'

'I told you, I don't know, but I can find out.'

The two men went back into the kitchen, where there was a woman singing a song in Gaelic. Richie hadn't a clue what the words meant. The woman was middle-aged, sitting on a stool, her hands clasped on her lap. Her eyes closed as she felt the meaning within the song, her head moving backwards and forwards. It was as if she was in a trance.

Everyone listened intently. Her voice was haunting, and would put a shiver up and down your spine. When she finished, a round of applause burst out.

The girl by the wall with the green clothes was very taken by the song. Richie could see she was moved by it.

'The next person to sing please,' a voice said. 'Regina Bergin, you're next.' It was the girl at the wall. She stepped forwards onto the middle of the floor. As she began to sing, you could hear a pin drop as silence descended. Regina had the voice of an angel. Richie was spellbound. At the last verse she took out a tin whistle and played it. The tin whistle was haunting. As she finished the song, there were shouts of 'more, more!' Regina slipped back to her spot at the wall.

All eyes were on Richie as he made his way over to her.

'That was beautiful, Miss Bergin. You have a lovely voice.'

'Thank you, sir,' she said with a shy smile.

'Will you try the next dance with me?'

'No, sir,' she said. 'I am going soon; my father is over there by the fire, and he won't stay long.'

'Can I meet you for a chat sometime? I would really like to hear your voice again.'

'Not until there is another social evening here, or in Brennan's. Anyway, there are lots of nice singers here; you haven't heard them yet. Breda Malone will sing and play the melodeon. She had a lovely voice too. There are many in the district that come to the dances and perform.'

'Next time then,' said Richie.

'We'll see … don't wait for me.'

Disappointed, Richie withdrew. 'Goodnight, Miss Bergin. I hope we will meet again.'

He was approached by two ladies who were much older than Regina. 'We will dance with you, sir. Or we will teach you how to do the set dance.' Out they went into the yard. The light of the moon made it almost as light as if it were daylight. They had an old man with them, and he was to jig along the music. They placed a glass of water by his side so his throat would not dry up. 'Diddle I die die, diddle I die,' the man kept going chanting.

Richie was finding it hard to pick up the steps. The women were patient and kept going until he got it.

'Now come back in with us and we will do the set.'

Another man joined them on the floor while the ladies called to the musicians for a set. The crowd clapped along to the music, as the dancers hurtled around the floor, dispersing the cloud of pipe smoke that had settled in the middle of the air. Once again, Richie began to feel light-headed from the swinging movements. Out of breath, he made it out to the yard, where he bent down with his hands on his knees for support as he breathed in the night air, perspiration running down his face and neck.

'My God, these people know how to wreck a man.'

The session did not end until daybreak.

9.

Richie let the O'Keefes know about his new car, which was due to be delivered in a month. He offered his car and his time to the O'Keeffes to take the journey into Limerick twice a week to visit the hospital.

'It will be a much quicker journey for you both, and more comfortable. Hopefully Aoife will get better and return home with you.'

Aoife had been in the hospital for more than a month, and did not seem to be getting any better. She was still sleeping heavily. The family were not sure if it was the medication she was under. Bernadette, though, saw a glimmer of hope on her last visit to the hospital. She noticed a twitch in Aoife's right eye. She kept talking to her and asking for a reply. She pointed it out to Harry, who said that it was nothing and that he could not see any improvement at all. He did not want to get his wife's hopes up. Bernadette disagreed, and reminded him of all the prayers that were being said for her recovery. Harry remained unconvinced.

On leaving the hospital that day, the nursing nun sister called the O'Keeffes into her office. It was the same office next to the ward Aoife was on.

'Take a seat,' she said loudly, and Harry thought somewhat unkindly.

The O'Keeffes sat with worried looks on their faces.

'What is it?' Harry asked the nun. 'Do you have any good news for us at this time?'

'No, I have not,' she replied with her head in the air. 'There is no good news in this section of the hospital. Ninety-nine per cent of patients never leave here, except in a wooden box. The doctor, Ned, did his rounds this morning. He is concerned that Aoife may be with child. Her belly is growing. He did some tests, and we will know more in a month's time. Meanwhile, we will keep her medicated and as comfortable as we can. It will be God's will if she is or not. There is nothing we can do, only hope for the best.'

The O'Keeffes were stunned, and could not reply or ask questions.

'Any questions?' the nun asked.

'We will have to ponder on this,' Harry said.

Bernadette was in a daze. She was so looking forward to Aoife marrying and having grandchildren, but not this way.

'What can we do, Harry?'

'Jesus Christ, woman, I don't know what we can do.'

'It can't be this way …'

'Even if she has a baby, she won't be able to look after it. It will be a torment to us all, knowing that it was by the British soldiers. The child won't have a chance in the world.'

'Don't think about that now, Harry,' she said. 'Wait until we come back next month. Maybe it's all false. Maybe it's not happening at all. It couldn't be.'

'The doctor said that it is.'

'Oh, the poor child,' Bernadette cried.

Richie and Tom were waiting at the hospital gate for the O'Keeffes. The O'Keeffe's had agreed to stay quiet on this and not tell anyone. When they found out for sure things might be different, but for now they kept things to themselves and were not planning to tell anybody anything.

Richie and Tom asked after Aoife's health. 'She is the same way,' they both said together. 'Although, I saw her eye twitch,' Bernadette said. Harry repeated, 'That's nothing at all. That would happen anyway.'

Bernadette was not so sure. She explained to Richie and Tom that when she kept talking to her and asking for a reply, she saw that happening.

'God is good; that's what I think,' she said.

'If God were so fucking good He wouldn't have let this happen in the first place,' said Harry, under his breath but still loud enough for everybody to hear.

★ ★ ★

Tom kept hanging around with Richie, driving him here and there. The fact that Richie's own motor car would soon arrive had not escaped his attention, and he wondered if that would be fatal to their friendship. Tom loved the role as a chauffeur, and relished the attention they were getting. Richie's American accent seemed to work wonders with the ladies, and it did Tom no harm to be associated with this exotic foreigner.

Richie heard of some land for sale just outside Bruff, and he went and had a look at it. It consisted in five acres along the roadside. The land was overgrown and in need of a lot of work. Tom advised him not to get involved in buying land because he would make many enemies.

'The neighbouring farmers would want to buy this land. Whoever is selling it must be in a bad state for money, otherwise it would never come on the market.'

Richie wanted it, however. What would Miss Fitzgerald think when she heard that he owned a piece of land from her own home town? 'She would just love that,' Richie told Tom.

'If she is as clever as you say, she knows it's impossible to buy land in a close-knit community. What are you going to do with it anyway?'

'I'm not sure yet, but I am thinking of building a small home there. Nothing too fancy; a place I can call my own here in Bruff is all. I intend to stay here for a year or two. Who knows, I might meet the woman of my dreams.'

'Jaysus, I thought you might do that,' said Tom. 'I knew by the head of you at the dance in Byrne's that night.'

'Did you now?' Richie enquired.

'What kind of a head had I for you to think that?'

'Ah, you were too interested in Regina Bergin. Many a man has her in mind, but she will not say yes to any of them! Maybe she was waiting for you to come along, eh? Saving herself for the right man. She is a fine-looking woman and a talented singer and tin-whistle player. Have you heard her play the harp?'

'No, but I would love to hear that. Does she play anywhere we could attend?'

'Next Sunday at early Mass she will play the harp.'

'What time is Mass?'

'Seven in the morning.'

'I will be there,' said Richie.

★ ★ ★

The O'Sullivan family had taken to Richie and treated him like one of the family. It was the only hotel or boarding house in Bruff. Richie had a routine going where he rose early and went to bed early. Soon he wanted something to do every day, so he discussed the Brotherhood with the O'Sullivans. He wanted to join them in the fight for independence. He felt that if he was doing something with the men that in some small way he was helping Ireland.

He had written to his father and let him know his intentions. The letter took weeks to arrive at its destination, and then it took even longer for the reply to reach Ireland. Eventually, though, a letter came. Richie's father was in favour of Richie joining with the Brotherhood in the fight for Ireland. The letter stated that his father was ready and able to finance the purchase of guns and any other armour they needed. Dynamite was in short supply and was a very important commodity in fighting for the cause. He had encouraged some business people in Boston to help out with finance. There was so much money at the ready, Richie asked the hotel owners again to get him introduced to the Brotherhood. He explained how he had met some of the men already, but that they had moved on and he did not know where they were now.

'Leave it with me,' Liam O'Sullivan said. 'I'll get someone to come forward and talk with you. I'm sure they will be delighted with any help they can get!'

O'Sullivan warned Richie to keep silent as there were British all around just waiting to hear of something like this.

'God knows what they will do to you if they get wind of anything. Keep everything close to your chest, otherwise you will draw attention on us here and that could result in a battle between us and the British. A man could lose his life over this, and many have.'

A bit taken aback, Richie agreed to silence.

'Don't you want to see Ireland free?' he asked Liam.

'Sure I do, but not at the cost of any lives being lost.'

The huge British army barracks that towered over Bruff was only a stone's throw away. Captain Rutledge was notorious for pulling up passers-by and sticking a sharp metal hook into their heads for no reason whatsoever. He was so brutal that everyone kept well out of his way.

Passing by the towering barracks, day or night, you were taking a chance. No one trusted that Rutledge fellow. Some people said he was not human the way he behaved with the Irish people; they felt like scoundrels when he was around.

'We know all's fair in love and war. Keep it at bay, that's what I think,' said Liam.

The injection of money to buy arms was welcome news for the members of the Brotherhood, and gave them renewed hope. Quickly, Richie was known the length and breadth of Limerick. He was the biggest celebrity that ever came to Bruff and Limerick. Even so, he did not go to his head and remained well grounded. It was the most natural thing for him to do what he could to help Ireland.

Liam O'Sullivan got in contact with the local branch of freedom fighters, and made arrangements for Richie Fitzgerald to meet them in the back room of his hotel. The hotel was busy that night, which kept the attention away from anything going on behind closed doors. Liam and Richie had a drink in the bar before heading to the back room, where the door was left open for the men to enter.

When the time came, the men appeared out of nowhere. They sat at the table with Liam and Richie. As Liam introduced Richie, the men were silent and somewhat nervous. It looked as if they were unsure of Richie. Liam O'Sullivan assured them that this man Fitzgerald was genuine, that he wanted to help, and that he could provide arms, or at least the money with which to buy them. Dynamite was the popular request from the Brotherhood. You could see the smile in their eyes with such an offer. It was like a dream come true.

The leader of the men, Bernard Fitzgerald, spoke for the men and agreed to get arms across from the USA. He explained that a lot of planning would have to be done before they would arrive in Ireland.

'We are being watched at all times, so this shipment needs to come in in the dark of night at some small island off the County Cork coast, where we will have men ready to unload the ship. Small boats will go along the side of the ship and take it off. Lookouts will have to watch from the Cliffs and down at the shore. A huge amount of planning will have to be done. It will take some time to get everything planned and safe. Then we take it in through the underground tunnel, and leave it in storage there before we move it on again. Whatever ship they come in on will have to be in sympathy with the cause.'

Richie had worked out a code with his father back in Boston. Only a few weeks had gone by when his father had the arms ready, and it only remained to find a ship that was willing to carry the cargo and remain silent. His father had many offers of arms and ships. The support overwhelmed him. When word got out in Boston of the move to ship arms over to Ireland, they had so many offers of armoury that they hired two ships. It turned into a huge operation. Volunteers stored the armour to look after it until it was ready for shipment. Secrecy was paramount among the volunteers. There was a lot of dedication and commitment and loyalty from every man and woman that was involved in the operation, both on the American and on the Irish side of the plan.

After one month, the shipment was on its way to Ireland. The contact with the ships was intermittent, which worried the men. Nevertheless, every man waited with excitement for the day when he would take up arms and fight with all his might to free Ireland, Richie Fitzgerald

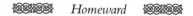

amongst their number. And perhaps he would not have to wait for long. Word reached Limerick that trouble was brewing in Dublin and that something big was about to happen.

10.

*M*eanwhile, the O'Keeffes were visiting Aoife once a week. Bernadette could see a little improvement in her; she said she noticed her listening when she spoke to her. Even so, she remained in a coma-like state. Harry thought it was the medication the doctor was giving her to keep her quiet, but he didn't hold out much hope of her ever fully recovering. It was heart-breaking for Richie to to see the family suffer; life would never be the same again for them.

On one of their weekly visits the nursing sister called them into her office. Without hesitation, she demanded a huge sum of money for the care of Aoife. The O'Keeffes were shocked at the amount. They knew they would have to pay, but this would destroy them entirely.

'There is no way we can come up with that kind of money,' Harry said. The most we can manage is maybe five pounds a week, and even that would not be easy.'

'Useless,' the sister said. 'We have looked after Aoife for more than a month; you already owe us over £100.'

'I could buy another farm for that!' he pleaded with the sister.

The next words out of her mouth totally shocked the O'Keeffes.

'Your daughter is with child.'

Stuck to the chairs, the O'Keeffes could not speak. Harry looked at Bernadette; tears were quietly rolling down her face.

'That's the worst news you could possibly give us.'

The sister's eyes were cast down. The news did not seem to faze her.

'How hard can you be, Sister?' Harry pleaded with her.

The sister did not reply. Her weapon was the silent treatment. In this hospital the nuns were very religious. Even so, they could most definitely put the fear of God into anybody who crossed them.

Harry and Bernadette were silent for a moment, digesting this information. Harry then stood up from the chair.

'Come on, Bernadette. We will be back next week and will bring as much money as we can.'

But Bernadette was not ready to go yet. She had questions that needed to be answered.

'Sister,' she said in a low voice, 'is she healthy enough to have a baby?'

'God knows,' the sister replied.

'Has she any idea she is with child?'

'No.'

'And what will happen to her?

'If you pay your bill here to the hospital she will stay here. We will decide what will happen to her when she gives birth. That's it now,' the sister said. 'Go home and think about this. I will see you both next week.'

Bernadette told the sister about the novenas being said twenty-four hours a day for Aoife.

'That can only help,' the sister said. At last they saw a bit of nature in the sister.

As they both walked down the hospital corridor, a heavy weight fell on them. The news they just heard was devastating.

'It was bad enough before,' Harry said, turning to Bernadette, 'but now to have a child, and especially by the bastards. Where is God at all? Aoife is suffering enough already. Who knows if the baby will be healthy or not? How come this is happening?'

He looked back to Bernadette again, and her eyes were filled with tears. She was choking back the pain, but was unable to find any way to contain it.

'If the baby is born healthy I will look after it for Aoife. It isn't the baby's fault … what happened, I mean. I will take care of Aoife too.'

★ ★ ★

The O'Keeffes could not come up with the money to pay the hospital. Harry knew that before he sat down and discussed it with his family. They were in deep trouble. It turned out that they had rented the farm from the landlord and were already struggling to keep up the payments. The landlord was a lenient man who knew well how hard it was to keep up the payments, and he had given them more time to pay when he heard of the terrible news of the rape of their daughter, but even so, their financial situation was quickly becoming desperate.

Harry seldom discussed financial matters with the other members of the family, and preferred to keep them to himself. Why worry them when they could do no more than they were already doing? But at this point he felt he had no choice but to let them all know what was going on.

That night, after dark, he called the boys to the table, which was dimly illuminated by a flickering oil lamp. Bernadette was already sitting down, saying the novena. With some papers in his hand, and sitting at the head of the table in his chair, he began to tell of how they were doing financially.

'We are in arrears,' he said.

'How much, Dad?'

'More than £118.'

The boys were surprised and shocked.

'But Dad, we are making good money with the milk at the creamery. We sold pigs just last week!'

Bernadette said that she had egg money and butter money saved, and would give it over to Harry.

'That won't go very far at all,' he said, without looking up from the table.

Now the family were wondering if they would make enough to keep the family home and farm. Harry had a suggestion.

'We could ask the Yank to help us.'

Silence.

'I don't want to ask anyone for help, but I have nothing else I can do.'

The kitchen door swung open with an enormous gust of wind. It blew the papers all over the place. It also fanned the fire, which sent smoke and ashes all over the kitchen. Bernadette stood and walked slowly to the door, looking outside to see what was happening. It was so quiet out there it was eerie. She returned to the kitchen.

'There is nothing there, nothing at all.'

'There is some angry spirit around here. The same thing happened when the Yank came to the house for the first time. Do you remember? Harry said.

'Ah, that was not the first time,' Bernadette said. 'That happened twice before when you were away at your sister's farm. I didn't want to tell Richie about that because he is from America and wouldn't understand that at all. Although he asked me about the sprit in the house, I said there was nothing here; that I didn't ever see or hear anything. I didn't want him knowing that there is something of a supernatural experience happening here.'

'Well it can fuck off and leave us alone now. Unless it wants to help with the bills so.'

Tom suggested that Bernadette should go to the shaman, Griffin, and seek get his advice about the spirit that lives in their home. She was reluctant to confess such a thing to anyone, and explained that the spirit was doing no harm to anyone of the family. Harry disagreed.

'Take a look around you, woman. What happened to our daughter?'

'The spirit did not do anything to Aoife; it was the British soldiers who did this!'

'I make the suggestion that the soldiers were way out of their territory that day they came across Aoife.'

'Nonsense,' replied Bernadette, 'they have been around here for the past few weeks. Not many people saw them, but they were there. They probably waited under cover until they got someone and tortured them. Those men would stop at nothing; they regard us Irish as animals or the scum of the earth. That's enough of that talk,' Bernadette said while getting up from the table.

Harry beckoned her to sit down again. She did so reluctantly.

'What have we to do now?' she asked? 'What happens next?'

Harry said he would ask the Yank again for enough money to pay what they owed to the landlord. Just then they heard the sound of a motorcar.

'Who could this be?' the boys remarked.

Within a few moments Richie Fitz was knocking at the door while entering the kitchen, a big smile on his face. He could see immediately that things was not comfortable in the house, even though they welcomed him in the usual way. After joining the family sitting at the table, he asked them if everything was okay.

'No, it's not,' replied Harry. 'We are in deep financial trouble here. We are way behind in our rent to the landlord. The hospital is looking for a lot of money for Aoife's care. I'm afraid we are going under. We were discussing what action we would take when you came. Maybe you came at the right time, Richie Fitz.'

Richie suggested that the O'Keeffe family should perhaps ask Harry's family for help.

'Ah Jaysus,' he replied, 'whatever we have they have nothing at all.'

Harry explained that he knew what happened to tenants who could not come up with the rent.

'We will have to walk out of this house and live on the side of the road like the tinkers. Only the tinkers will have a tent; we won't have anything.'

Richie Fitz sat in silence, listening to the torment this family were going through. Bernadette butted in.

'That's not all; we have news from the hospital about Aoife. The hospital wants payment too, and it's completely out of our reach. The nun called us in to her office, and didn't hold back on anything. She wants payment for Aoife's stay. Back payment for the past month and each month from now on.'

She held back the news of the baby, trying to keep it within her own mind, although she knew what was facing her and the whole family. Bernadette prayed and asked God not to be so cruel, she asked all the saints and angels in heaven to help the family.

The kitchen table, once a hive of activity and love and laughter, had become a sad and lonely place.

Richie felt it too. Without hesitation he offered help with everything.

Harry spoke whilst staring up at the ceiling. 'Somehow I think you were sent here to us, the spirit of your forefathers

called you to your ancestral home. And now you are here
and willing and able to help us. That first night you came
to visit, that gust of strong wind that opened the door and
blew the fire and smoke around the room was a sign of the
spirit, although I didn't think of it that way then. Pondering
on everything, I believe you were called back here.'

'Ah no,' Richie said, 'it was my great aunt Trudy
Fitzgerald in South Africa enticed me to come. Then I got
obsessed with coming to Ireland and finding this home
here.'

'Taking that into account, it could still be the spirits,'
Harry said.

'Well I don't want to upset the spirit that lives here, is
there any way we can connect with it? So that I can let it
know I mean no harm.'

'That's not the way it works,' Harry replied. 'Whatever
the spirit wants, it will not stop until it finds peace.'

'Well how can we find peace for this spirit?' Everyone
looked at Harry to hear his reply. A long loud sigh from
Harry. 'I don't know for sure yet; I have to consult with
someone.'

Now everyone sat in silence. After a moment, Richie
spoke.

'Try not to worry too much. I will come back tomorrow night and have some news about the finance.'

'You are a gentleman,' said Bernadette. Harry nodded
in agreement.

'We are so grateful for your help.

All that night Richie pondered on the O'Keeffe
family. He wondered about how best to help them out.
Considering they were in financial trouble now, with payments overdue and their daughter's hospitalisation, what
would be needed to remedy the situation? No one knew.
Questions kept popping up. He could find no real answer

to their plight except to offer financial help, but that was not a long-term solution. One thing for sure was the care of Aoife.

He decided to send a telegraph to his father back in Boston, briefly letting him know what was happening in Bruff. He needed advice. Although his father had no real concept of the situation, he would for sure want to help out, especially when it came from his son, in whom he had great faith.

After breakfast Richie headed up the street to the post office to get the telegram off to his father. It was a nice bright sunny morning. The post office was quiet—not a soul there. He waited for the postmistress, who by this time he knew well, to come to the counter. However it was not her this time but an elderly woman with a shawl around her, snow-white hair all tied up in a bun at the back or her head. She had a pair of rose gold hoop earrings embedded in her earlobes, which looked like they would never come out of there. Her face bore deep wrinkles like tracks. Her eyebrows were sticking out, some black and some white.

'Oh, so you are the returned Yank?' she said.

'Well I don't know about "returned", but I am here for some time.'

'I am the post office assistant's mother. I ran this office for many years. I am just standing in for her today. I hope you are not going to ask for something difficult for me?'

'Nice to meet you, ma'am,' he said, extending his hand in friendship. She had a warm, tight handshake.

Richie pulled his notes out of his pocket.

'I need to send a telegram to my father in the USA.'

'Oh, that will cost you a bit,' she said.

'Not to worry; whatever it is it will be okay with me.'

Looking at the note, the old woman said, 'Fitzgerald, that's your name?'

'Yes, ma'am, that's it.

Laying her arms on the counter, her face scrunched up and looking Richie straight in the eye, she said, 'Would you be one of the Fitz's that lived near Lough Gurr?'

'Well, they are my ancestors. That's why I am here.'

'I thought so,' the old woman said. 'I remember an old man, Dick, lived there. He died alone. His mind had left him.'

'That is him,' said Richie. 'He lived like a recluse I believe for the last years of his life.'

'He had a shotgun by his side, and wouldn't allow anyone into his house. I think he was afraid of everyone and didn't thrust anyone,' she said. 'Many unusual and terrible things happened in that house. It was before my time, but I heard stories being told about hangings and killings going on there. He kept that shotgun beside him at all times. The old man had married twice. His first wife died tragically. It was the local parish priest who made a match for him with this young woman. Being so young, she was a powerful worker around the place. But he was old, and not able for the bedroom happenings. Young wife or no, he was not hungry for her, although he did give in on some nights, now and again. He must have, because they had a baby, which was of course the talk of Bruff. This old man having a family again, when his first family was already grown up, one of them married and with children himself.' She shook her head, disapprovingly.

It began to dawn on Richie. Could the child be his aunt Trudy in South Africa? He kept it to himself.

'Many a neighbour talked about hearing him shooting. Some even wondered if he were trying to kill himself.

Others thought he was shooting at a spirit that dwelt in the house. Or maybe he just liked to shoot; in a strange way that was the only power he had over anyone, frightening anyone that came near the house. Some said he was demented. Close neighbours that knew him well felt sorry for the man they once knew as a kind and helpful neighbour. But by then they were not sure how he would take it if they went near his home. They often remarked how good a neighbour he was, and he was kindness itself. Who knows how he became such a recluse, or how he had survived there alone in the house.'

She was deep in thought, lost amongst her memories. 'Well, we can't bring the dead back.' With those words she stepped back from the counter. 'Wait, wait a minute,' she said. She walked back towards the office behind her, and went down on her knees to open a safe. Dust flew everywhere. She pulled out a pile of envelopes or letters that were held together with a piece of twine. She coughed as she walked back to the counter. 'Here,' she said, holding the pile of letters out to Richie. 'These belonged to Dick; the postman could not deliver them to him. With the rifle and all. The postman was nervous and thought he might be shot.'

'Well, ma'am, I wouldn't know what to do with these letters.'

'They are here in this office for many years. You are here now and a descendant or member of the family, so I want you to take them. I don't care what you do with them; they are yours now.'

As she began to attend to Richie's own communication to his father, Richie looked at the dusty letters in his hand, then quickly put them into his pocket. As he walked out the post office door he heard screams from outside the military barracks. There was this British soldier whipping a young man. Richie stood watching, stunned. Surely this could not go on like this forever? It had to stop.

As Richie walked on past the barracks, trying to keep as far away from the ordeal as he could, he chatted to six or seven men standing at the corner of the street. Mostly they were there to get some work from farmers who needed a labouring man for the day. They gathered there every morning hoping to get a day's work.

★ ★ ★

Back in his room, sunlight beamed in through the windows as Richie sat on the side of his bed. He took the letters out of his pocket and laid them on the bed beside him. Personal letters from his family maybe? Some were brown envelopes. Some had the Crown seal—government letters perhaps?

His thoughts stopped him from going straight in and opening them. It didn't feel right to open up his ancestor's private letters, so he picked them up and placed them in the bottom drawer of his dressing table. He had other important things to do on this day. He got his new car ready and headed out to the O'Keeffe home.

He was greeted with the usual welcome, Bernadette putting the kettle on the fire; Harry sitting on his chair at the head of the table.

'Sit down, sit down,' said Harry, gesturing to the chair at the other end of the table. 'It's good to see you, Richie.'

'I am here to help you,' replied Richie. 'I can't give you any long-term solution, but I want to do what I can. There is a lot to consider here. Your sons and your daughter, how they are going to survive without enough money coming in from the farm? These landlords … are they keeping the rent themselves?'

'Ah no,' Harry replied, 'it's all for the British. The land-lords are only collecting it and then handing it over to their boss, whoever that is.'

Richie struggled to make sense of the situation.

'Aoife is our first concern,' he said. 'We need to come up with a plan and make sure she has the right care in the hospital.'

'That's all we want for her,' Harry replied.

'Whatever happens we must pay the hospital and keep the treatment for her. How do you intend to manage on the farm, Harry?'

'I have no plan because I have no money ... unless I rob a bank!'

'Stop that talk,' interrupted Bernadette. 'Rob a bank? What will you think of next?'

'I have sent a telegram to my father. He might know what do to. Although I think I know what he will suggest,' Richie explained. 'Let me visit the hospital in Limerick and explain to the nun that everything will be paid in due time. I will reassure the sister of payment. Let's start by making sure that her treatment continues.'

Richie saw torment in the faces of Harry and Bernadette.

'Please do,' Harry replied. 'Next week we will go to visit as usual, and you will have a chance to talk to the sister.'

'I will do what you say,' replied Richie.

'That's settled then,' said Harry. 'You are the kindest man I have ever met.'

Despite Richie's offers to help, Harry looked some-what crestfallen as he stood up to shake Richie's hand.

Bernadette set the table and made some tea and soda bread along with the butter she had churned yesterday. She had some gooseberry jam, which tasted good with the bread and butter.

With the tea over, Richie stood and announced that he was going, but would return the next day.

Harry and Bernadette sat by the fire after the milking and yard work were done. Both sat in silence for a while. Bernadette broke the silence.

'That's a great man that Richie Fitzgerald.' Harry stared into the fire. 'I don't know what will happen to us, but I do know one thing: he will help us whatever way he can.'

'I believe that too,' said Bernadette. 'We will have to tell him the news of the baby.'

'Wait a minute,' said Harry, 'hold on about that.'

'It's only right we let him know.'

'We will tell him in time.'

'What do you mean "in time"?'

'I hope to get the bill paid first, then we will consider telling him that news. Jesus, I don't want to have to tell anyone that news.'

'Well, it's there now, and there is nothing we can do about it.'

'Maybe God will take it. The child would be better off with him. Who knows how it will turn out to be?'

'Stop that talk, Harry,' she said. 'That little baby did no harm or will do no harm to anyone. It is not the fault of the baby. It's Aoife and the baby now.'

'How can we live with this?'

'I don't know, but I do know we will have to deal with it.'

'Another thing … what about things for the baby? Like a cot, or bed clothes …?'

'Hold your horses there now, you're losing the run of yourself. We will have to prepare.'

'That's a long way off,' said Harry. 'We don't have to be thinking about that now. We have to pay the bill and see how we can keep her there in care until she comes around or has the child.'

A stern look crossed Bernadette's face. She exhaled pointedly. 'These things have to be planned. We may not like where we are, but we have to deal with it. There is really no choice about that. I'm the one who will have to look after it. That is, until Aoife gets better. I have a good feeling, and I think she will come out of that when the baby arrives.'

Harry was not happy at all with the way his wife was talking about the baby. That was something he did not want to think or talk about. He felt so angry, and, worse, he felt helpless. His only daughter had been destroyed by these men. The situation with money only made things worse. Harry was a proud and determined man, and everything had been taken away from him. This situation shook him to the very core. He looked into Bernadette's eyes.

'Leave it so now, woman.'

She knew that the conversation was over for the moment.

11.

*R*ichie arrived back in Bruff, and stopped to talk with O'Sullivan for a moment or two, asking him about any progress with the Brotherhood.

'All quiet at the moment,' he replied. 'I will let you know when I hear anything.'

The bundle of letters was on Richie's mind. He sat on the edge of the bed in deep thought about the O'Keeffe family and how best to help them. He decided to wait for word from his father.

Opening the drawer in the dressing table he pulled out the bundle of letters. He removed the twine and laid the letters out on the bed. There were more letters then he first thought. It was difficult to make out the dates of most of the letters. At least four were from South Africa. Of course they were from his great aunt Trudy.

He was reluctant to open them. He knew they were personal letters between father and daughter. He began to sort through the rest of them, turning them over in his hand.

There was a knock on his bedroom door.

'Mr Fitzgerald?'

'Just a minute,' he replied, gathering the letters and placing them back in the dressing table drawer. Opening the door, he was confronted by a telegram boy.

'Are you Mr Fitzgerald?' the boy asked.

'That's me.'

'A telegram for you, sir. Please sign here.'

Richie signed and sat back on his bed, opening the telegram, which was from his father.

> *Son,*
>
> *Do whatever it takes to help the O'Keeffes. We cannot see them in such trouble. At least keep a roof over their heads and take care of their daughter. If possible get her into a hospital in Dublin. I'm sure they have more up-to-date care available there. I am forwarding on a money order which you will collect at the post office. Most of all, take care,*
>
> *Your Dad.*

Reading it through again, Richie reasoned that it was out of the question to send Aoife to Dublin. She would be too far away from her family, who could see her only once a week as it was. What else could be done, though?

He came up with a suggestion for Bernadette: perhaps they could take her home? With loving, tender care from her mother and family, maybe that would be more useful to Aoife than being tended to by the nuns, whose main motivation seemed to be financial rather than spiritual. Surely being in her own home, being in familiar surroundings with her family, could be beneficial? If they brought her home, they could then emply a part-time nurse to help administer what drugs she needed, and he would be able to take care of the financial burdens that came with that. He resolved that he would put it to Harry and Bernadette when he saw them tomorrow.

He was lying back on his bed with his arms behind his head, pondering the situation, when his thoughts were interrupted. Without any warning, five or six shots of gun-fire deafened his ears. Richie jumped out of his bed and looked out of the window. Men were running down the street, jumping into the river and swimming downstream. Close behind them were two British soldiers firing at them. As far as Richie could make out from his vantage point, they did not succeed in killing the men, who were quickly out of sight.

It was a shock to watch this incident happening. Richie went down the stairs and spoke to O'Sullivan, who said he knew nothing; he heard and saw the same as Richie. Quietly, he told Richie that it may have been some of the Brotherhood taunting the soldiers to get them to follow them while they had men ready to enter the barracks.

Still a little shaken up, Richie decided to take a walk down by the river. A man he didn't know stopped him, telling him, 'Don't go down by the river; there is trouble there and you don't want to be in the way of it. You could get caught up with the men and be killed or maimed.'

Richie thanked the man and returned to his bedroom. There was no sign of O'Sullivan about at all. There was no one behind the bar, which was unusual. Richie listened for a few moments; the place was eerily quiet.

Suddenly men came in from the back of the bar, and grabbed what looked like hiking bags, threw them on their shoulders and left quietly. O'Sullivan was standing at the back of the room. He shook the men's hands as they left, and spoke to them in Gaelic, which meant that Richie had no idea what was been said.

Coming back to the bar, O'Sullivan told Richie the men running and the British soldiers after that was a decoy to allow the Brotherhood to come and pick up their belongings and get out of Bruff safely.

'But men could have been shot or drowned in the river!'

'That was the chance they had to take for the plan to work out. They were all fine anyway; no one was shot today. There is something big going to happen in Dublin shortly. Don't breathe a word of that,' he said to Richie, 'or you will have us all killed here.'

'I would like to be in on the plan,' Richie said to O'Sullivan.

'That won't happen. The men are trained in what they do, and you have no knowledge of that training. Tactics and fitness, good with explosives, and a good shot—it all takes time, my friend. Nobody can just join and then go to war and fight the British. We have to leave all that to the powers that be. They know best what to do in this situation. Will you have a drink?

'I'd like a glass of water.'

'Ah, for fuck's sake, will you have a decent drink to mark this occasion?'

'I don't know what the occasion is,' replied Richie. 'Water is fine for me; I am thirsty is all.'

'Well I am having a large whiskey. Will you join me?'

'Okay,' replied Richie. 'A small one for me please. It isn't really my thing.'

O'Sullivan toasted Richie, and grimaced as down the hatch the whole glass of whiskey went. Richie thought it best to leave now and go to his room.

Early the next morning, just after sunrise, Richie cranked up the engine on his new car and headed out of town to the O'Keeffe's household. On arrival at the bottom of the lane to the big house, Richie could see Harry in the field bringing in the cows to be milked. He was alone. When he heard the noise of the car he stood and waved, then resumed his work.

The O'Keeffe boys were ready with the milking buckets scalded and prepared to take the milk. Richie left the car parked up and went to the door, where he found Bernadette in her usual spot, cooking breakfast over the fire.

'I'm making some gruel,' she shouted to Richie. 'Your name is in the pot.'

'Good woman,' he replied.

'Sit down there at the table; it won't be long now.' Bernadette seemed quiet.

'How are you?'

'Well I don't really know how I am at the moment. My head if full of thoughts, and I can't seem to quieten it down. There is so much to think about, and I am not sleeping at all. Harry is the same. We are devastated, Richie. There's nothing else for it. What are we going to do at all?' She turned and looked at Richie.

'That's why I'm here. I have a proposal for you and your family. It would be better if I talked to you together.'

'This is the thing that upsets me most. We were always able to handle anything that came before us, but this is just awful. Poor Aoife. My heart breaks for her, but we can't stop … we have to keep everything going all the same. Harry finds it hard to accept what happened and stay quiet about it. It's shameful for a man to have his daughter violated like Aoife was. Then we don't know if she will ever come out of the coma she is in. We will have to beg, borrow or steal to find a way to pay for her care at the hospital. Then I wander off into thoughts, like what will happen to her when we are gone? How could there be a God up there with the likes of this happening to Irish people? I'm sure Aoife wasn't the first person this happened to. It's a very lonely place to be. I feel alone with this burden. It's a heavy load on one woman's shoulders.'

Richie sat in silence and let Bernadette pour her heart out. She obviously needed to share her feelings with somebody, and perhaps it was easier to do so with a relative stranger than with her family. He could understand that.

Turning to look at Richie again, she could see that he too was upset. His eyes were red and watery.

'I wish I could make all this go away for you and your family. I am praying for you too.'

'We will wait for Harry to come in, and then we can talk about everything.' With that, she returned her attention to the pot above the fireplace.

After a while, Harry came in and sat down in his chair. Bernadette put bowls of gruel in front of him and Richie. One of the boys came with a jug of fresh milk.

'Put a few spoons of sugar on that and it will taste much better,' Bernadette advised.

Harry had almost spilled half the bowl of sugar on his gruel.

'The sweeter, the better,' he said to Richie, pouring the fresh milk into the top of the bowl.

After some time, Richie broke the silence.

'This gruel you make, Bernadette … do you buy it at the local shop?'

'Ah I do, Richie, a big sack of it at a time.'

'How is Aoife doing?'

'The same,' replied Harry. 'No change at all.'

'Now and again I can see a glimmer of hope in her,' said Bernadette.

'That's what you think,' Harry said. 'You must be serious about this. No one else sees anything going on, only you.'

'A mother knows best. It's there, I have no doubt. She is changing because you know she is with child.' Bernadette put her hands to her mouth as if to retrieve this truth, but now it was out in the open. Harry was stunned, and leaned his head heavily upon his hands, his elbows on the table.

'Oh Jesus above help us, help us. Our daughter is violated by the bastards, and now she is going to have their child.'

'It's not Aoife's fault!' Bernadette shouted in a high-pitched voice. 'She didn't do anything wrong! It's what happened to her.'

Richie spoke in a calm voice. 'We can do something about it. Leave things to me for a while. We can work out something. We will make plans to visit Aoife tomorrow, and I will talk with the nun about her care and the care of the baby.'

Richie stood and shook both their hands. Harry felt it difficult to accept any gesture of help; he was the person the whole neighbourhood would come to for advice, particularly on land rights and boundaries, neighbouring rows or upcoming court cases, of which there were many. He liked the fact that people came to him for advice, and had spent many hours sitting at his table going through all the details of the problem at hand, recommending they come back with more information. He left no stone unturned. And liked it better when things turned out as he had suggested. People would come back and relay how things went, often bringing some kind of thanks. Once a young calf was brought to him; on another occasion a kid goat. Big sides of pork when they had killed a pig. Everyone was grateful for his good advice and help. The situation now was of course he needed help, but was to ashamed to ask for it. He felt he was letting himself and his family down. He felt this too much to bear.

Richie's offer of help did not sit well with him either, but at least no one would need to know about that. Harry fully intended to ask Richie to keep it amongst themselves.

Richie agreed to silence. Harry assured him that one day he would be in a position to repay his debt. It was important to him not to be indebted to anybody.

'I don't want to leave this earth owing anything to anyone.'

'Nonsense, Harry. Tell me this: how can a friend be in debt?'

Harry was moved by this generosity from their American visitor. But no reassurance from Richie would deter Harry from wanting to repay him. Richie knew that this was unlikely to be the case, but was content to carry on the fiction that he would be repaid to salvage Harry's pride.

The work on the farm continued as ever, but now attended by silence. The laughter and levity had left this place.

12.

Richie left the O'Keeffes', reminding them that he would return early the next morning for their trip to the hospital.

It was late in the afternoon when Richie returned to Bruff. As he drove into the town there were many people hanging around. He stopped at the street corner and asked one man what the crowd was waiting for. 'Nothing that I know of, sir' was the reply. Richie lingered a bit longer, hoping that someone would come forward and let him know the truth.

Eventually he moved on in the direction of O'Sullivan's, where there were more people standing. He parked outside O'Sullivan's, but found the pub to be eerily silent. Not a soul was in there.

Richie recognised O'Sullivan amongst the crowd. 'O'Sullivan! What's going on? What are we all waiting for? Nobody seems to know.'

'They know all right. They are not going to tell you is all! Sure you're just a blow-in.'

'Why? Everyone in this town knows me now.'

'They know who you are, but they don't know you as a person.'

'A "blow-in"? After all this time?'

'Ah, don't mind that. You can be here for fifty years and still be a blow-in, sure. It's the old lady in the post office.

She's in her final hours; everyone is waiting for word. She is well known here for her position in the post office; her daughter runs it now.'

'I met her last week.'

'Well, this came on her suddenly. Her family is followed by the banshee; we're waiting to hear her cry.'

'And how does this "banshee" know anything about this old lady? And why would she care?'

'Sure our culture is different from yours, Richie. It's widely known about the banshee and who she follows.'

'Can't say I've ever heard about her.'

'It must be only in Ireland.'

'I suppose. She would hardly travel to America to follow the dead.'

'Almost everyone believes in her, but there are a few that say it's only a wild hare that you can hear bawling.'

'Do you believe in this?' asked Richie.

'I do! It's our heritage! When we hear her we know that she has the soul of the person; that they have left this world.'

'To hell with the "banshee". Does she follow the Fitzgeralds?'

'She does,' O'Sullivan replied gravely.

'What about my ancestors who passed away here? Did she come for their souls?'

'For sure. That old man, Dick, was dead for a long time before he was discovered. She had a free hand with him I'd say. Nobody would have heard her out there in the back of beyond.'

Richie was stunned. 'What about my father in Boston do you think she would know if he passed?'

'Ah, I doubt it. She would never go that far.'

'I was only talking to the old lady in the post office a few days ago. She seemed fine to me.'

'She got a heart attack yesterday and didn't come out of it. The doctor said it is just time that will take her now.'

The old lady passed during the night. O'Sullivan heard the banshee, but decided not to talk to Richie about it. The Yank did not seem to understand.

For the next three days, the wake continued. All the while people were coming and going from the house. The old lady was laid out in a white satin and lace shroud, rosary beads intertwined between her fingers. Her white hair was neatly combed back behind her ears. Her earrings were still embedded in her ears. She was whiter than the whitewash paint on the wall. Some of her family sat by her side at all times. The conversation between her relatives and the locals always made complimentary remarks on how she was kindness itself. Those who knew her well cried all the time.

Tea and cake were served by the ladies of the town while the men got a drink of strong whiskey and food if they wanted it. A group of about six or seven men stayed there day and night, periodically bursting into song. Some fell asleep sitting upright on their chairs.

It was an eye-opener for Richie, as in Boston most remains were cremated as there was not enough room in the graveyards, although he remembered looking through an old graveyard that had headstones dating back almost one hundred years. All had Irish names on headstones that were now tilting sideways.

Richie hadn't thought how his father would want to pass on. He resolved to discuss it with him when he returned to the States.

Richie waited around the bar, reading the weekly newspaper. He heard what he thought was a loud high-pitched screech. O'Sullivan stood up from his chair.

'Oh Jesus. Another screech as loud as the first one. You heard that, didn't ye? She is gone all right, Lord have mercy on her soul.' He blessed himself with the sign of the cross. 'She was a good woman, worked hard all her life and brought up four children, all on her own. Her husband, John, died years ago, and she has been on her own ever since. It was no bother to this woman to get on with life and what life threw at her. She will surely be in heaven.'

The men that were standing around all came into the pub, ordering rounds of porter. 'Paying respects to the dead,' they said. All of them spoke in hushed tones. Until the porter started taking effect.

At bed time, around eleven o'clock, the whole pub was heaving with men. Then it turned into music and song, all with respect for the post mistress's passing. There was no going home until morning came. When daylight appeared outside, someone shouted, 'It's daybreak; come on home now.'

Two old men sat on a stone outside the house, chatting and smoking pipes. Richie noticed how quietly spoken they were. They were not having any drink, just cups of tea. Clearly these were the wise men of Bruff.

Approaching them with outstretched hand, Richie introduced himself.

'Good day, sir,' one of them said. 'What brings you here?'

The men listened intently as Richie, a little the worse for drink, explained his presence. The men looked at one another for a moment, then one of them said, 'Did that ould fella leave any money behind him, or was it all down the Swanee?'

'I don't know anything about that,' replied Richie. 'I don't want to know either.'

'Maybe the leprechaun came back for his pot of gold!'

Loud laughter ensued between the men. Richie stood, not knowing what to make of this thing called a leprechaun. Miss Fitzgerald had not told him anything about this mythical person.

'Ah Jesus, they are not mythical; they are real small people who dress well and have much gold, especially at the bottom of the rainbow!'

'Stop codding me, guys. You know I am from another country and don't know all the happenings here with your banshees and your leprechauns. You men are full of superstition is all.'

'Don't kid yourself, man; this is true, and you better believe it, otherwise you will come to some harm.'

'Really? I may be a blow-in, but I've been here for long enough to see what the problems here are, and they have nothing to do with banshees and leprechauns. That's just storytelling for children.' Porter had provided Richie with resolve. 'The British have crimes to answer for here, and these ghost stories have nothing to do with that.'

'Don't be too quick to dismiss these things now. The banshee could come looking for your soul. You should be careful what you say. If you stay around here for too long, you may just end up believing in her yet.'

A bit shaken up with all this talk of the supernatural or mythical stuff, Richie bade farewell. Glancing back over his shoulder he could see the two men sniggering.

With no sleep whatsoever, Richie made his way slowly in his new motorcar to the O'Keeffes' home, where Bernadette was ready to go. There was, however, no sign of Harry.

'Where is the boss man?' enquired Richie.

'Some of the cows are gone missing; he is gone to find them. It may take a while depending how far they have gone, so he told me to go ahead with you to the hospital and not to wait for him.'

'I thought it would be better if the two of you were there to sort out Aoife's care and what to do next.'

'I am fine to go with you,' she said. If you don't mind, that is.'

'Not at all, Ma'am; we can do this together.'

On the drive to Limerick they chatted about what to do for the best, but concluded little. 'Let's see what they suggest,' offered Richie.

'We can take it from there, sure. That's settled then,' replied Bernadette.

Entering the hospital was a strange experience. Richie was very aware of his surroundings, the highly polished floor glistening with the sunlight, the wooden staircase highly polished too. There was a smell of Jeyes fluid, which was used to disinfect everything. Bernadette was silent beside him.

The first landing was the same, the sun shining in and illuminating the building.

'You would never think there were patients here with mental problems. It looks so sterile and clean.'

'Peaceful, even.'

That was it until they entered the area where Aoife was. Richie could see Bernadette's face going white.

'Are you okay?' asked Richie.' He could tell that Bernadette was somewhat lost without her husband beside her, for it was he who made most of the couple's decisions. It made her courage all the more remarkable. Courage or no, though, she felt uncomfortable without Harry there. She felt that he should be there with them, supporting her and Aoife. Was it possible that no cow had gone missing and that the real reason why Harry was not with them was because he did not want to face the nuns without their payment? It didn't seem like him, but the pressure he was under might have made him do things that were not in his nature. Maybe he just couldn't take any more requests for money and felt that he was just about ready to snap.

'I don't know what way I am going to find Aoife today.'

'Come on; let's find out.'

He pulled the bell-cord, but it took a long time for anybody to come to the door. Someone peeped through the blinds on the glass window in the door, then opened it. They were taken straight into the nursing sister's office, where they sat and waited some more. A tray of tea and biscuits arrived for them, 'compliments of the sister', according to the maid who served them.

'They have never given me tea before, when Harry was with me,' she said. 'It's because you are with me this time and the nun is trying to make an impression; she must have seen us come in.'

After a while the sister duly arrived, sat down at her desk and pulled out a file.

'How is Aoife?'

The sister did not answer the question directly. 'Who is this man beside you today?'

'This is a friend of the family. He came from America to visit his ancestral home.'

'Richie Fitzgerald, Ma'am.'

'Are you related to the Fitzes from Bruff?'

'I am. Do you know the family?'

'They had connections to the Fitzgeralds from Kildare. I'm afraid that one or two of them went mad and ended up in places like this, but you probably knew that already.'

'Yes.'

'I started my nursing career in Kildare. I remember some of the family. They were rotten in money, land and gold, and they didn't know what to do with it all.'

Richie detected that the sister was interested in how much money he had, and whether she might be able to persuade him to part with some of it. For Aoife's sake, he went along with it, though he wasn't happy about it at all. What choice did he have?

'I don't know that my family are "rotten rich", but we have some investments.'

'We are here to see Aoife,' prompted Bernadette, 'and to come to some arrangement about her care.'

'Well now, Mrs O'Keeffe, that's going to be a problem for you. It looks like she will have this baby in five months' time.'

'What have you decided about that?'

'We haven't had time to come to some arrangement yet, but I will take care of the baby and look after Aoife too if that is possible. We won't be looking after it here in the hospital. There is a mother and baby home here in Limerick. I don't think she will be suitable for this establishment. If she was up and about and able to carry on herself ... well, that would be different. At present she is unable to look after herself. It's only for the dedicated nursing staff and skills that she is as good as she is. Who sent in the money order yesterday evening?'

Bernadette looked at Richie, whose face showed surprise.

'What money order?'

'It was delivered here with a telegraph through the local post office. There was no name on it; it just said "For the medical care of Aoife O'Keeffe". It is a lot of money: four hundred pounds. We are paid up until the baby is due, when she will be transferred to the lying-in hospital for the delivery of her baby. I will take you to the ward where she is; follow me.'

Walking quickly, she led them through corridors and up stairs until eventually they came to door number fifty-five.

'Come,' the nun said, 'sit beside your daughter. There is another chair for you, Mr Fitzgerald.'

This time she was in a smaller ward with just one other bed, which was curtained off.

'Poor Aoife!' Bernadette cried out. 'What are they doing for you at all?'

Richie could see that Aoife was highly medicated. He noticed, though, that when Bernadette spoke to her directly her eyes focused with a stare. Richie suggested that Bernadette speak directly to Aoife, and when she did the same thing happened. Richie was convinced that there was something there. Perhaps some small recognition of her mother's voice. He didn't want to get her hopes up.

'Do you see any sign at all in Aoife? I think she knows my voice. She knows I am here.'

'Yes, I'm sure of it. I have seen that twice now.'

Bernadette kept on talking to Aoife, asking her questions, and also letting her know how things were at home.

On leaving, Bernadette kissed Aoife on the forehead. Aoife jumped up in the bed and started screaming. The nurse ran into the ward and immediately gave her an injection. After a few minutes she quietened down and fell asleep. Richie was sure that she would come out of the coma-like state she was in. He spoke to Bernadette on the stairs on the way out.

'I believe your daughter will recover; it's going to take time. I noticed when you made contact with her she got upset. That I'm sure is connected with the ordeal she had. She just needs some time is all.'

'But how much time?'

13.

Harry was not in the least bit impressed at the nun's suggestion for his daughter. 'The mother and baby workhouse in Limerick? No fucking chance of that! It's only down-and-outs and the poorest have to go there, and then they have to give up their child for adoption.' He puffed on his pipe contemplatively. 'Maybe that may not be a bad thing for Aoife though. She would be rid of it then.'

'Stop!' Bernadette shouted to Harry. 'How can you say such a thing? I won't agree to the workhouse, never in a million years. Aoife is our only daughter; she would die in that place. She would never come home from there.'

Harry did not reply to Bernadette. He knew Bernadette was right; Aoife wouldn't last a week in the workhouse. Some serious decisions needed to be made.

Richie sat silently and did not interrupt.

'And what money did the holy bitch want from us this time?'

'No need to worry any more about money for that sister, or Aoife's care. Some anonymous person sent a money order in full payment and payment for the foreseeable future.'

Harry was shocked. 'What do you mean, money order?'

'It came through the post office in Bruff.'

'Divine providence … is that what you are telling me? I don't know anyone with that kind of money do you?'

'Well, no.' But someone paid, thought I don't know why.'

Harry threw an eye Richie's way. 'Was that anything to do with you?'

'Well it was not me personally, but my father in Boston. I had told him what had happened here in this home. His ancestral home. Without question he volunteered to send a money order to the hospital. He could not stand by and do nothing. Any word from me and he will do what he can.'

The energies in the O'Keeffes' kitchen seem to feel a lot lighter. Help for them was out there, somewhere. Harry sat in silence, dumbstruck. He was digesting what he had heard. No words could be found; everyone was surprised or shocked.

'Jesus,' said Harry. 'That's a sign from God he is working for us and helping us. He would want to hurry on; we don't have that long before Aoife gives birth.'

Harry sat back in thought again, pondering.

'I am thinking about this little child that will come into the world. Could it be healthy at all? The father, whoever he might be, could be off his head … he probably is to do such a barbaric thing to another human being. De we even know if she is only having one child? Could there be multiple babies there?'

Bernadette was silent; she had never considered that there might be more than one.

'The sister would have said if there was more than one. They can tell by now, can't they?'

'She is on a lot of medication,' said Richie. 'And she might be better off without it.'

'The nuns might not agree to that, though. They just want the patients in their care to be quiet; they don't treat them properly, not really,' said Harry.

'That might be right. They do what they want to do, and there isn't a lot anybody can do about it.'

'I visited a neighbour once at this hospital,' Harry said. 'I'll never forget it. The men went around in a terrible state, some of them out of control, some of them shuffling about sideways, mouths open, drooling on their clothes. It was mayhem. The people who were meant to be looking after them were just interested in controlling the crowd. They would lash out at them and beat them when they felt like it. Sure, who was to stop them?'

'They aren't all bad, Harry,' offered Bernadette.

'Well I'll tell you this: Tommy Moore didn't recognise me when I went to see him there. Thirty years I have known that man, and he had so much of their "medication" it was like he was possessed, like he was terrified of everybody and everything. His clothes had not been changed, and he smelled. I'll never forget the way his eyes were popping out of his head. He kept on scratching his head, and blood was running down his face. By the time he got out of there, the man I knew was just gone. He was a fine man.'

'He was. And a good uncle to his brother's children. He worked day and night to help his brother, Joe.'

'By the time he got out ... gone, just gone. It's a mad house in there, I tell ye.'

'Why was he put in there in the first place?' asked Richie.

'He started seeing and hearing things that weren't there. Then he started shouting things and being a nuisance to everybody. The hospital was the only place where they could put him.'

'And Aoife is there now. We can't let it continue like this.'

'Well, the powers that be turn a blind eye to the goings on there. They just give out whatever medicine they like, that's what I've heard about it. God knows how many of the patients end up in the River Shannon at the back of that place. Suicides … or not.'

Harry began his ritual of tapping out the pipe and refilling it.

'I got the cow. She had strayed into the Dillons' farm and across to the wood. I got her just before she made it in. I would have had a hard job to get her if she had gone in all the way. That quarry at the north side of the wood would have took her; many an animal has fallen in there never to be got out of it. Maybe the spirit was calling her. Anyhow, she is in the milking parlour now and she is safe. If we lost her we were finished altogether.'

Richie nodded in agreement. Bernadette was silent.

'I'm going in to get the kettle boiling and make the tea.'

'We are starving.'

'Ah, sure, ye are always starving when I get home. Ye haven't a hand to wipe your rear end.'

'That's right, Missus,' replied Harry.

Richie walked in directly after Bernadette.

'I will help you, Ma'am.'

'Not at all; this work is for the woman of the house. That's my job and my place here.'

After an hour or so she turned up a fine meal of rashers, onions and spuds. You could smell the onions frying way down the yard, tempting everyone to go in for dinner, but they knew to wait for the call from Bernadette. Only when the dinner plates were filled with food would she call them in to dinner.

Harry, the sons and Richie wolfed down the food with lashings of fresh home-made butter melting over the spuds, while Bernadette just picked at it. Mugs of fresh milk from the cows went down a treat. His belly full, Harry once again began to fiddle with his pipe, cutting tobacco.

The sky outside was heavy, yet a ray of sunlight defiantly shone through a crack in the dark clouds. A loud clap of thunder shook everywhere, followed by a sudden streak of lightening, and then the sky opened with heavy rain, which continued for a good twenty minutes. Then the sky cleared and you could only hear the thunder in the distance.

They went outside into the yard. Everywhere seemed clean, the trees glistening and the grass damp with rain-drops. Freshness came upon everything.

'It's nature's way of clearing the air around us and freshening up everything,' Harry said. 'It's a fresh start, a new beginning, if that's possible.'

'God is good,' said Bernadette, gravely.

'And the Devil is trashing. Our mother used to tell us that God was angry and was throwing everything around in heaven, making noise so that everyone would know that he was angry with the world. Mother said that it was us he was angry with. We must behave and be a good family otherwise he would get angry again!'

'Ah stop will you?' she said. 'Don't be thinking that way; have a bit of faith.'

Harry walked over to the cowshed, his head down, kicking at the ground as he went. Richie and Bernadette went back into the kitchen.

'Sit down there now,' said Bernadette, 'and we will have another cup of tea. I am so thankful to you, Richie, taking me in to visit Aoife today and your father so kind-hearted paying the bill, I don't know what I can do in return for you.'

'You have done enough, Ma'am,' he said. 'Just being here in my ancestral home and meeting the O'Keeffe family is enough for me. Anything I can do for you and your family, I will.'

When Richie drove back to Bruff he decided he would continue on into Limerick and visit the hospital unannounced.

★ ★ ★

When Richie arrived at the hospital reception there were no staff there. He checked around to find someone, then decided instead to climb the stairs and go straight to the room they were in earlier that day. No one was in sight; the doors were unlocked and there was not a sound anywhere. No shouting or screaming like every other day when he came with the O'Keeffes.

The quietness was eerie. Looking back over his shoulders now and again, he moved forwards with trepidation. Just then he heard footsteps. He stopped and heard them again. It was coming from a room at the end of the corridor. Richie moved back and ducked down behind the huge pillar, where he waited, hardly breathing. Out came the priest of the hospital, fixing the belt of his trousers. He passed by swiftly, down the stairs and into a door marked 'private'. Unsure of what he had seen, Richie moved on to Aoife's room. She was there, standing naked, cleaning her private parts with a towel. She continued to put her nightgown on. Obviously, the priest had molested her.

Richie was furious. How could a man of the cloth do this to a sick woman, or to any woman? This man should not be a priest. He needed to be taken out of the hospital and defrocked. Put into gaol and never let out again. Gaol was far too good for him.

'How are you Aoife?' Richie stepped into her room. I am here to help you.'

She looked towards Richie, remaining silent. she got into her bed closed her eyes and seemed to sleep. No one came to the ward, and everything was quiet, not at all like it was in daytime visiting hours.

Richie looked closely at her, but there was no movement in her closed eyes. Leaving the room, he walked down the corridor glancing into the wards where the doors were open. All the patients were in bed and sleeping.

Down the big staircase and on the ground floor he heard some chanting. Peeping through the keyhole he saw many nuns with their rosary beads running though their fingers. The door at the back of the room opened and out came a priest in his Mass vestments, the most beautiful robes with white and gold details and it flowed to the ground. With a swagger he turned to the altar behind him. He spoke in Latin while the congregation replied in Latin. This was evening Mass, and the man doing the service was the very man that was in Aoife's room a few minutes before.

A young woman, dressed in white, moved past him and into the church. Through the briefly opened door he caught a smell of incense and of candles burning. The floors were highly polished in the chapel and would squeak if you did not lift your feet.

Coming to the end of the Mass, the congregation sang hymns. It was time for Richie to get out of there. Walking out the door un-noticed, he headed for his car. He pushed it down the hill so he would not be heard starting it up.

During the drive back to Bruff, Richie hardly saw the road in front of him as his mind was trying to work out what he just saw. There were so many questions and no real answers. What would he tell Aoife's family? Was she drugged so that she could be trapped there for Father Brendan's use? Was the baby she was carrying his?

14.

*H*ow could God let this happen to this young woman? Attacked in the fields, and now raped again in this 'hospital'. It got worse every day. Now something had to be done for this young woman, and sooner rather than later. It just couldn't carry on any more.

Richie decided that he would talk with O'Sullivan in the morning and ask about the hospital and the sisters there. O'Sullivan considered it to be a good hospital. 'It's where many families put their demented children or siblings. Anyone that goes in there never comes out, as they are not fit to live outside the hospital. They are a danger to themselves and everyone around them.'

'Do you know anyone in there?' Richie asked.

'Ah, I do and I don't,' he said. 'Some have passed away in there and you would never know about it as the families abandon them and don't want to know anything about them. Sometimes you would hear about a young person going in and maybe the workers there would let it slip that they died. There is a burial ground, or cemetery as they call it, in the hospital, and they are all buried there. Those poor people are to be pitied; the nuns have a vocation; I don't know how they look after so many of them.'

'Sure you know the O'Keeffes' only daughter is in there? That poor family are heartbroken.'

'The hospital is the only place for her.'

Richie listened with surprise. My God, he thought, if O'Sullivan doesn't know the truth then nobody here in Bruff knows what is going on there.

'Why are you asking me about this?' said O'Sullivan.

'Just wanted to know about the hospital as we have many in Boston too, but not as many inmates there I don't think. I am interested to find out if Aoife O'Keeffe is in the right hospital for her as she is very young and is there with much older women. It doesn't seem right for her.'

'Ah no,' said O'Sullivan. 'Sure there is nowhere else for that young woman. She will get used to it like them all. Well I have never been in there,' he said, 'I'm going on what I hear about the hospital. Thank God none of mine are there. Some families here in Bruff and I'm sure everywhere are cursed with this disease of the mind. We call them lunatics or imbeciles. They are born with this affliction.'

'There are many women there, and I'm sure they could do better than they do in that hospital.'

Richie walked away and out into the morning sunshine. There was a stillness over Bruff. A quiet, clear morning. No British Army about. Not a sign of the Brotherhood. Everyone seemed to be sleeping in.

Ever since the previous evening, Richie had been in a state of heightened awareness. It was time he called to the O'Keeffe household. On the drive out to the homestead he was unsure of how to let the family know what was happening at the hospital. Would they believe what he was about to tell them? The fact that O'Sullivan knew nothing of the happenings there un-nerved him. How could it be that O'Sullivan, who knew everything and all the happenings that went on in Bruff and most of Limerick too, knew nothing about this? He had connections everywhere; he was clever man. And yet surely there was no reason why O'Sullivan would lie about the hospital.

On arriving at the O'Keeffe's he was greeted in the usual friendly fashion. Yet he could see the sadness in their eyes. Bernadette, in particular, had black circles under her eyes; they were not nearly as bright as when he first met her. Harry was looking shaken too. Richie was aware of the torment the family were going through. He could not muster up the courage to tell them about the hospital and what he discovered the evening before. He felt the heart-break before he said anything to them, but he felt that he had no choice in the matter: they simply had to know what was going on in the hospital. He sat and chatted with Harry while Bernadette busied herself with making the brown bread.

Feeling a bit uncomfortable, he quickly decided to leave. Harry and Bernadette tried to make him stay for dinner, but he did not want to. He breathed a sigh of relief when he sat in his car. He decided to return to the hospital in Limerick and confront the sister. Even that was disturbing him. Common sense prevailed, and he continued on.

On arrival outside the hospital he decided on his strategy; he would find the sister or ask for her at reception. The receptionist was cheery and friendly. 'Mr Fitzgerald,' she gushed, 'what can I do for you today?'

When he asked to talk with the sister, the receptionist responded, 'I don't know if she is on duty today. Please take a seat, sir, and I will find out for you.'

Richie thought this odd as she was always here every time he came with the family. After several minutes she returned. 'Sorry, sir, she is unavailable at this moment, but if you return tomorrow at noon she will see you then. Otherwise I can take down details of your visit and pass it along to her later today.'

'I want to talk to the sister now!'

'Sir, she is not here today; there is nothing I can do for you.'

'I'm sure the woman is here; she never leaves this place. Go and get her this minute.'

Reluctantly, the secretary walked back upstairs and closed the heavy door behind her. Richie could hear a loud voice, 'Tell him I'm not here, and won't be here for a week. Go down and tell him now.'

Hearing that, Richie climbed the stairs two steps at a time. The secretary was just leaving. Richie held the door and burst in. There she was.

'What are you doing here? You have no business talking to me about a patient's welfare. You are no relation to any person here in this hospital, so go now before I have you thrown out!'

'That's where you are wrong, Ma'am.' Richie stood and put both hands on her desk. She moved back a tad. 'You must have no knowledge of what is going on here in this place. Because if you do, you are allowing an awful thing to happen. This place is a disgrace!'

'You don't know what you are talking about, young man. The care in this hospital is the best in Ireland.'

'Jesus, if that is so, there is no hope at all.'

'Get out of my office or I will call the police.'

'Not until you answer my question.'

'I do not have to answer any of your questions. I already told you, you are not related to any patients here at this hospital.'

She dug her heels in. She was furious.

'Aoife O'Keeffe is not the scum of the earth; nor is any other patient in this hospital.'

'Sir, will you please leave my office?'

'How many people leave here with a clean bill of health?'

'I will not answer you.'

'That's because no one ever leaves this place. Do they? They come here to die, sooner or later.'

'I swear I will have God himself damn you. I will put a curse on you. Then you may come here for help from me.'

'I would kill myself first! You know that I know what you are doing here. You look the other way while your clergy visit these poor women's rooms and have their way with them as often as they like. I saw the priest with my own eyes. You know it, and have done nothing.'

'I don't care what you think you know, Mr Fitzgerald. Of course our priests need to visit the rooms to hear confessions, or to administer the Holy Communion. The clergy attached to this hospital are men who have time to listen and have sympathy with our patients. And I would suggest you keep your accusations to yourself in future.'

'And they take advantage of young women. She may be even carrying this priest's child!'

'What you are saying is a sacrilege. Priests don't father children. I know nothing of this, and I dare say you cannot prove otherwise.'

'I am making a formal complaint about what I witnessed here.'

'Formal complaint? To whom?'

'I will have the police here with me today and close down this place.'

'Any complaint, formal of otherwise, will come to me. And now you have made your complaint, so you can leave now, and I will investigate it.'

'You have not heard the last of this.'

Richie left, with many thoughts running through his head. He kicked at the dirt under his feet as he walked to his car. How could this place have been able to get away with this? If they were treating Aoife like that, who knew how many other women had been subjected to the same?

★ ★ ★

The next morning he arrived at the O'Keeffes' home with a determination in his voice. He would tell the family of his concern in the hospital.

123

As he entered the house he heard someone chanting and a reply in a man's voice. He entered and saw Bernadette and Harry down on their knees with the beads between their fingers like he saw the evening before at hospital with the nuns. They both lifted their heads and kept praying the rosary. When finished they greeted Richie with open arms.

'We were praying to God for help with everything.'

'Yes,' Richie said, 'I have seen this praying before, actually only yesterday evening at the hospital. Can we sit for a few moments? I need to have a talk with you.'

'Wait a minute,' said Bernadette. 'I will fill the kettle and have it on the boil for the cup of tea.'

'No need to do that,' Richie said.

They both knew at that moment that Richie had something serious to talk about.

'There is no easy way to tell you what I saw at the hospital yesterday evening.'

They listened intently as he gave an account of his unannounced arrival at the hospital, and what he saw in Aoife's ward. All Richie could see was shock on their faces. Both were stunned at what they heard; neither of them spoke. Richie looked at Harry straight in the eye and asked the question.

'Did you know anything about this behaviour with the priests?'

'No,' replied Harry. 'I did know that they did things with altar boys who were too young and ashamed to tell their parents. One of those boys was my elder brother, Thomas, who got sick and died of tuberculosis. The poor man had no life; he was sick most of his adult life. He had told me about the priest and what he was doing to the boys after Mass. This was so shameful that he swore me to secrecy. If I told anyone it would bring shame on the family and our mother and father would not believe him anyway. Not only to the family but somehow the boy would be at fault himself, making him out to be the instigator then he would be a shame to the family. I would not be an altar boy even though my parents wanted me to do it. They wanted me to join the priesthood; I was the one earmarked to join. Most big farmers had a son earmarked and a girl to join the nuns. None of my family did: my father told all of us that we were pagans; we would bring shame on his family as he himself had two sisters who were nuns and one brother a priest, Father William. He was sent out to the missions somewhere in Africa and never returned. I suppose he died out there from some sort of disease.'

What can we do to help our daughter?' said Bernadette, hardly able to speak. She looked directly at Richie, and then turned to Harry. Silence descended.

'I have a plan in my head,' said Richie. 'I have been thinking about this all night long. I will go back again this evening at the same time and see what happens, then we will know if it is an everyday occurrence.'

'No,' Harry said. 'Once is enough to see our daughter treated like an animal by a priest. And the British soldiers!'

Richie told them his plan to remove Aoife from there.

'I have made an arrangement to visit the sister and Aoife at noon tomorrow. The three of us will go together and take her out of there. I will go to your doctor here in Bruff and let him know what we intend doing. Hopefully he will prescribe the medicine Aoife needs.'

He looked at Bernadette. 'Prepare Aoife's room and get it ready for her return home.'

A slight smile came over Bernadette's face she blessed herself with the sign of the cross. Harry was not so sure.

'How will he be able to provide the care she needs? She needs doctors, nurses, medication …'

Bernadette disagreed. 'I will give her everything and all the care she needs. You know I will, Harry. Those people aren't helping her, only themselves.'

'What about the child?' continued Harry. 'Do any of you know if the child is the bastard's or the priest's?'

'We don't know,' replied Richie, 'and I suppose we will never know. This thing may have being going on with the priest the day she arrived at the hospital.'

'How can the sister and her staff let this happen to anyone?' asked Bernadette.

'They are very hard people; that sister probably never wanted to be a nun in the first place. She was probably put in there like my two sisters. That said, in the eyes of God … how he could allow this to happen to anyone?'

'That sister can burn in hell for all I care about her,' added Harry.

'We will go at noon and see the sister as usual in her office. Who knows how Aoife will be.'

Harry and Bernadette hurried and got ready to leave with Richie, instructing their two sons to take care of everything until their return.

As they drove along the country roads, Richie made conversation. Harry knew the owners, if not the entire family history, of every farmstead they passed by. Richie was curious to know how they survived the famine or how they made payments to the landlords.

'Ah sure, they are all struggling like ourselves.'

The conversation seemed to dwindle away when they got near Limerick City. You could feel the tension.

★ ★ ★

On arrival at the hospital they went together to the reception, where they were greeted in the usual formal way.

Only today they were ushered into a room just left of the reception desk. It looked similar to the room where they usually waited for the sister. There was the same kind of big desk, and the same kind of window behind it. Only two chairs occupied the room. They were strategically placed in the full light coming in the window.

Richie asked Harry and Bernadette to sit; he would stand behind them. Only a few moments went by before the sister entered the room. Standing behind her desk she looked quizzically at the three people.

'I was only expecting to see Richie today,' she said.

Harry rose to his feet

'Sit down, Mr O'Keeffe; no one stands in front of me in my office. You are required to sit at all times here with me.'

'Not this time,' Harry retorted. 'I will not sit in front of you ever again. We are taking our daughter with us today. We will leave here and never return.'

Red-faced and shaking, she replied, 'This will not happen in this hospital. Once you are committed here that's where you will stay until you pass on to the next world. You signed the commitment form in front of me the day you brought your daughter here to this hospital.'

'I signed no papers for you; you don't have my signature on any form here. I will swear to this in any court of law in this country.'

'Mr O'Keeffe, I have the forms to prove it. Everybody knows that I run this hospital and that everyone is signed in here before they are admitted and committed. You and your family and your new American friend cannot and will not remove this patient from here. You will make yearly payments and can come and visit. But your daughter will not leave here.'

'Ma'am,' Richie said, 'we have come to take Aoife home. We do not want any confrontation with you or the hospital here. We can assure you that she will be well taken care of in her home with her loving parents.'

'You will tell me how to run my own hospital, will you? Mr Fitzgerald, you know nothing about our procedures here. It is most certainly not your business or your problem.'

'You are a fucking bitch,' said Harry, now furious. 'You are a Black and Tan supporter. You support the worst kind of people, the men who turn families out of their homes, the men who rape and beat women, men who do not believe in God or man.'

'There is no need for language like that, Mr O'Keeffe.'

'Holy sisters my arse. You will rot in hell!'

He pounded his fist on the desk. The sister just looked like it did not shake her at all.

'Let's go and see Aoife,' said Richie. 'Then perhaps we can all talk when we are calmer.'

'Calmer!' the sister shouted. 'I am as calm as balmy night with a full moon. It's the O'Keeffes who need to calm themselves and listen to reason. Nobody talks to me like O'Keeffe did just now. I can call the peelers and have you thrown into gaol and left there to rot. I will not have my good name and reputation sullied with the likes of him. You will not see your daughter today, and I will make it very difficult for you to see her in future. Get out of here before my patience with you runs out.'

'We will be back,' said Richie.

He opened the heavy door, and slammed it shut loudly behind them. Harry was furious. Bernadette was doing what little she could to calm him down.

'Harry, we mustn't make things worse.'

'Worse! By God, woman, how could things be worse?! Jesus Christ … who put this woman in charge of this hospital? She is not fit to mind mice at a crossroads, let alone be in charge of human beings.'

'Well now,' said Bernadette, 'this is her job. This is the way she does things. So we will have to go with her plans, for now anyway.'

'Never,' Harry said, 'I am going straight to Bishop Cleere. Maybe he can do something. Will you take us there, Richie?'

'You will have to have an appointment to see his holiness,' said Bernadette.

'Today I will try to see him, and if not we can make an appointment with him.'

On the way into the town of Limerick, they happened across Tom, the hackney man. Richie stopped the car and shouted at Tom. He asked for Tom's help with the visit to the bishop's house.

Tom replied, 'It's only the poor and down-and-outs and homeless go there to ask him for help. Are you all right?'

'The O'Keeffes have some major problems with the hospital their daughter, Aoife, is in.'

Richie explained what he saw the evening before, and then what happened this morning.

Tom asked, 'Were you seen coming or going from there last night?'

'One person saw me: a young nun who was late for prayers. I doubt if she would tell her superior as she seemed nervous about being late.'

'I wouldn't trust her at all. I'd say she did tell the sister. They do that to earn favours from their boss. Ah, she knew all right. Bishop Cleere most likely will take the sister's side in this; he is known for it. He will deny any wrongdoing on the priest's part; he likes to turn a blind eye to all of that. It's never spoken about, even though everyone knows it goes on. The bloody nuns can do what they want in that hospital and are never questioned about anything. The priests and the nuns work hand in hand.'

Listening to Tom, Richie couldn't believe what he was hearing, although he knew Tom had no reason to lie to him. His mind reflected back to the night before when he asked O'Sullivan the same questions about such things. His answer was so different.

Richie asked Tom if he could recommend anything they could do for Aoife.

'Let things lie for the moment and everyone will cool down. Then we'll get around to the matter of removing Aoife from there.'

'We don't have a lot of time,' Richie blurted out to Tom.

'What, is she going to die or something?'

'Oh no, she is with child.'

Tom stood still for a moment or two.

'How unfortunate for the O'Keeffes. Those bastards who did this should be shot. That lovely girl and only daughter ... violated by that lot.'

'That's not all, there is more, but I cannot say anything until I find a way to help the O'Keeffes first.'

'That hospital is not a suitable place to keep that young woman.'

'There is nowhere else for now,' Richie said.

Tom suggested to try the bishop anyway. 'Sure he can't make it any worse, so it's worth a try.'

Getting back into his car, there was a chill in the car. No sound came from the O'Keefes, who were lost in their own thoughts. They were clearly in shock.

Richie suggested they would go to the tea rooms and have a nice cup of warm tea. Bernadette loved the suggestion of warm tea, while Harry preferred to continue to the bishop's house. Richie agreed: tea first, and then to the bishop.

They stopped at Ahren's tea rooms, where there was a roaring fire and some comfortable seats close by. They sat and ordered a large pot of black tea with some scones and jam. It was delicious and felt warm in their bellies.

On the way to the bishop's house, Richie made suggestions on how to approach the subject of taking Aoife out of the hospital, Bernadette caring for her in their home instead. The sister had probably contacted the bishop already.

The bishop happened to be there in the house. The maid showed them into the parlour and sat them down on the chairs. There was a big fire in the grate there also. That felt warm and comforting. The room had lovely lush furniture with heavy curtains on the windows. Everywhere they looked there were portrait paintings of the bishops gone before.

Harry remarked on the smell of holy oils and incense. It smelt like Christmas Mass at home in Bruff. You felt full of the glory of God Almighty.

The maid stuck her head in the door and informed them that the bishop would see them and would be along in a few moments.

While they were waiting for him to come they heard the maid answer the door many times. People were in desperate need, and came to the house looking for anything they could get from him in the line of food and clothes. Mostly the maid turned them away, saying that they had nothing to give. Some people could be heard crying, 'We're just asking for a crust of bread for the babba, please. Or a drop of milk for the babba.' It brought it home to Richie just how desperate the situation was in Limerick. The people really had nothing. It saddened his heart because he knew well how the British had everything and wanted for nothing in the line of food and clothing and a roof over their heads, while the Irish, who had fallen on hard times because of them, had nothing at all.

The door swung open and the bishop entered, holding out his left hand where there was a large ring on his middle finger, a large ruby stone in its centre. Bernadette was the first to go and kneel in front of him and kiss his ring. Harry followed, and Richie did the same, although he didn't know why they were kneeling and kissing like this.

'Sit down now,' he said, 'and tell me why you are here.'

He was dressed all in black, except for his white collar and a purple scarf. He had a white beard, and his hair was soft and white, combed straight back. He had a mouthful of prominent white teeth. You could feel he was more than just a priest; he had that air about him. His ring had in fact been given to him by his holiness the pope. It was like kissing a piece that God himself owned and passed along down the line.

Richie spoke first, and requested that they remove the O'Keeffes' daughter from the mental institution and take care of her at home. There was a moment of silence as the bishop looked at Harry and Bernadette.

'Bishops are the guardians of all hospitals in the land,' he said gravely. 'Why would you want to do this to your daughter? Isn't she better off where she is at the moment? She will get the care she needs there with the nursing sisters.'

'That's the problem,' Richie sighed; 'she is not getting the care she requires at this hospital. We have spoken to the sister in charge about our concerns, but she can't see what's really going on there. That would be the charitable interpretation.'

'What do you mean "what's going on there"?'

Richie explained in short the happenings of evening before, he could see the bishop changing colour to snow white when he had told him all. He was clearly annoyed at this information about the priest.

'I don't believe what you say,' the bishop said. 'None of my flock will do something like this. This is the first time anyone has come to this house with such accusations. It must be the girl herself who is seducing the priest and tempting him in front of God. With your complaint I am bound to investigate this matter and talk with the chaplain of the hospital. Return in one week and I will give you my decision.

'But she could be dead by then,' said Harry, exasperated.

'I doubt very much that will happen. She is in the best hands with the nursing sisters there. I know what I have been told by you all, but you will understand that I have to investigate the matter myself. One week from today, return here to this house I will be waiting for you.'

With that he stood, then left the room, his cloak swaggering behind him. Before they left the bishop's house the maid came and asked for specific details about Aoife, her age, what date she was admitted there, her date of birth and so on. The O'Keeffes gave all the information about their daughter before departing the house in silence.

While driving home to Bruff they talked to Richie about the happenings of the day and how concerned they were about another week. All were upset about the idea that Aoife would have to stay there for another week. It could be even longer than that, of course, before they would be able to bring her home.

Richie knew that the locals like O'Sullivan would not help in any way, they turned a blind eye to the awful tragedy of young women. They had one obsession, and that was to free Ireland of the British. Every moment of time was spent organising the Brotherhood, collecting bomb material and armour. What was going on under their noses seemed not to concern them nearly as much. An attack seemed imminent.

As Richie dropped off the O'Keeffes he asked them to try and not worry too much as whatever could be done would be done. He assured them he would return in a day or two, and have hopefully some good news for them.

Good news had been, for the O'Keeffes, in very short supply.

15.

As the week progressed, Richie spent most of his time trying to figure out a way forwards for Aoife's discharge from the psychiatric institution. Every time he came up against a brick wall. He had nowhere to turn. He would have to wait until the end of the week and see the bishop again, although he did not hold out much hope of the bishop resolving the situation.

Coming towards the day to return to the bishop's house, he noticed a lot of activity at O'Sullivan's. There were a lot of coming and goings of the Brotherhood. The leader of the men recognized Richie and came to talk to him and thank him again for the arms he had organised from Boston and their safe landing in Ireland. They would come into good use fairly shortly.

Richie decided to ask for information about the situation with Aoife O'Keeffe's situation. Ruari Quinn listened to Richie, and then remarked that this was happening almost every day.

'People are being put into the poorhouse and they are no better off. Some of them contract scurvy and die, while tuberculosis is rampant in every institution. The place that girl is in is not the worst place at all. At least she is being looked after and is not hungry and dying like other places.'

Ruari advised Richie to leave things lie as they were, although he knew the family were devastated about their daughter and the place she was in now.

'There is more tragedy in Ireland. The British have inflicted 800 years of oppression on us, and it's time now to move forward and take back our country. Ireland's freedom is what we want and what we will fight for.'

He bade goodnight to Richie and disappeared out the back door of O'Sullivan's. Richie was half sorry for asking for help at all. He could see from this man Ruari Quinn that freeing Ireland was more important than anything else.

The logistics of grouping the freedom fighters under secrecy was a major task. However, he was involved with the O'Keeffes' problem, and committed to a resolution for everyone concerned. He was not convinced that the bishop would do anything to secure Aoife's release from the hospital. Somehow he knew that he would side with the sister and what she had said.

Bernadette was nervous. Her hands were shaking, Richie noticed. The bishop stood in front of her again with outstretched hand.

'Sit down, Mrs O'Keeffe. You too, sir.'

He sat himself in his green velvet, well-decorated and cushioned chair, his hands intertwined across his chest. He was silent for a moment, then took a deep breath.

'I have made enquiries with the nursing sister, and had a meeting with her and the hospital committee. Your daughter is not well enough to leave the full-time care of the hospital. She is not improving with what medication they have there. They are going to try her on another drug that will keep her quiet. This will give her a chance to rest and be more kind to her. You are a very lucky family; the sisters there are so very good and kind to your daughter. They understand your concerns for wanting her home.

She is not fit to leave this hospital, and maybe never will be well enough to leave. You must understand this. I have spent too much time on finding out about your daughter, which I don't normally do for any family. Seeing that you have paid up your bill to the hospital is a bonus. I have every faith in the hospital and the care given there. So, that's my conclusion.'

He stood and fixed his collar in a sign that the conversation was over, and left the room, his verdict delivered, without further ceremony.

The maid did not arrive this time, so they let themselves out.

Richie was not happy with the bishop. 'This man has blinkers on. He knows nothing of what is happening here at all.'

'He is a clever man,' said Bernadette. 'He won't admit to anything; he will back up his flock to the end. I think we will never get Aoife home.'

She started to cry.

She then apologised to Richie. 'Sorry,' she said, 'I … I just keep breaking down so much. Every door is closed to me. This was my last hope.'

'Never give up hope,' Richie said. 'Who knows what could happen? We will let everything lie for the moment. I will consider everything again. Hopefully I will find a way.'

It was near nightfall when they got back to the O'Keeffe's. Harry was waiting at the road gate for Bernadette's return. He was not hopeful that Aoife would be with them. He did not ask any questions, just greeted Richie and then put his arm around his wife and walked her up the lane to the house. Richie left and returned to his lodgings in Bruff.

However, Richie had an idea: he thought about going back to the hospital in the late evening like before and getting into the room where Aoife was. As he lay awake in bed, he hatched a plan that he thought might work.

★ ★ ★

Next evening Richie decided to return to the Limerick Mental Hospital. He parked his car away from the hospital so as not to make any noise. When he entered the front hall it was clear there was not a soul there. He went up the stairs to the room. Just as he got to the door he heard a noise. He ducked back and down the stairs, and proceeded to the rest room beside the empty reception.

With the door ajar he could see upstairs. After a moment he saw a priest coming out of the room, down the stairs and into the room that was for prayer.

Now it was time to take the chance again. He made his way up the stairs and into Aoife's room, successfully this time.

Aoife was lying on the bed looking up at the ceiling. He came close to her bed, whispering to her quietly.

'Aoife, your mammy and daddy want you to come home with me. Would you like to come home?'

There was no answer; her eyes closed and she seemed to sleep. Richie shook her shoulder. Her eyes opened, and she whispered, 'Take me home please.'

'We must hurry,' he said. 'Do you have clothes to put on?'

She shook her head.

'Well I will take the blanket from your bed and put it around you.'

All the while he was listening for noises or voices. He was pretty sure that all the nuns and staff were in the room praying, with Mass to follow. Just as he was all set to take Aoife into his arms there was a loud, severe screech from the ward next to Aoife. She froze and covered herself and would not move. Richie stood and waited for someone to screech again. Aoife seemed to know that something was about to happen. She still would not move. They could hear footsteps coming up the stairs. Many footsteps. Richie peeked out and saw four or five priests coming up the stairs. He knew what was about to happen, and so did Aoife. This was a Friday evening, and probably priests from the parish came to visit the women in the institution. The sister in charge had to know what was happening to the female patients.

There was nothing Richie could do now, just make himself scarce. The moment he knew that the men had gone into the wards of other women, he made a dash for the stairs, out through the reception and out the front door. He looked back; there was no one following him. He took a deep breath. It had been close. But he decided there and then Aoife O'Keeffe needed to be taken out of there as quickly as possible.

But how could he do it? He could not think of anyone he could turn to for help. That nursing sister had full control of the hospital and the patients there. What was he to do?

The happenings there seemed to be routine. Patients were being raped every day, and all in the full sight of an administration dominated by priests who conspired to keep it quiet. The O'Keeffe family would not believe it unless they somehow saw it with their own eyes. The people harming them were the very people they looked to for help.

Richie contacted his friend Tom the hackney man, and met with him the next day. Tom advised Richie not to interfere with the hospital.

'This kind of thing goes on, but everyone turns a blind eye to it.'

Richie pressed Tom for some way of resolving the problem. After a bit of persuasion, Tom agreed to help

Richie to go back again to the hospital and make another attempt to rescue Aoife.

That evening, both men brought their motor cars to the front gate of the hospital. They had a plan. Richie would go in again and quickly wrap Aoife in a blanket. If anyone came along, Tom would whistle three times. If he was caught in the hallway he would say he was there to see some patient.

This time it worked. No one came up the stairs and while no one came into the hall where Tom stood. With Aoife wrapped in the blanket off the bed, Richie came down the stairs with her in his arms. Quickly, both men went to their cars. Richie put the girl into the back seat of his car and covered her completely with the blanket, while Tom cranked up Richie's car. The car sped off with Tom close behind.

They went as fast as they could back to Bruff, and then up the road to the O'Keeffes' farm. Not stopping at the road gate, they continued straight up the lane to the house.

Harry and Bernadette were standing at the door. They could not believe their eyes when Richie lifted Aoife from the back seat. Harry and Bernadette took her and carried her into the house. Richie could see a slight smile on her face. Bernadette opened the bedroom door and laid her daughter down on her bed.

Harry and Richie with Tom in tow sat at the kitchen table discussing how they made the break with Aoife.

'If it weren't for Tom here I could not have done it,' Richie said.

He was so very happy that Aoife was safely home with her family. Harry discussed the possibility of the hospital coming to take her back. Richie suggested they did not let them inside the door of the house. He said they should have a plan in place if any of the hospital people came to take her back there.

'Over my dead body,' said Harry. 'I will have my gun at the ready and kill them if I have to.'

Richie disagreed with the gun; he recommended that they should treat them peacefully and talk with them first.

'We can say she is not here at all, that I took her to her aunt in maybe Dublin for treatment in the psychiatric hospital there.'

'That's sounds good,' Harry said. 'We will have to be alert to anyone coming up the lane from now on. I would find it very difficult to just talk to them with the terrible thing they've done to my daughter. I would prefer to spit in their faces first and then shoot them between the two eyes. Then shoot myself.'

'And then Aoife would have no father, and Bernadette would have no husband, and it would all be for nothing,' Richie said.

'The way I feel now I am ready to be punished, but I want justice for our daughter.'

'Even if it means they will hang you?' Tom asked, and then wondered if he had overstepped his bounds.

'I would get the Irish army to help me fight the bastards.'

'It's all right saying that,' said Tom, 'but the Irish army may not want to interfere with a family matter. You know that, Harry.'

'Don't worry, I will calm down. But I will never forgive those men. It will stay with me until the day I die. We must put our energies into the care of Aoife, get whatever up-to-date help for her there is. First thing is to get help with the delivery of the baby.'

After some time, Bernadette joined them at the table. 'She is fast asleep now,' she said. 'Hopefully she will rest peacefully tonight.'

She did sleep peacefully all that night until daylight came into the room. Bernadette had slept on the settle bed beside her. She woke when Aoife did. Aoife rose from the bed like she always did at home, and went to the toilet.

When she returned, Bernadette had a good view of her swollen belly. She observed Aoife, and came to the understanding that Aoife could be about six months with child. That would tie into the rape. She was guessing really as it was hard to know without a doctor's opinion.

Every day the O'Keeffes were waiting and watching for the police to come to the house looking for Aoife. But as the days went by, they never came. Nobody ever showed up to check on Aoife. Even so, Harry was always ready. His gun was cleaned and primed. He had it in his mind to kill anybody who came to the house wanting to take his daughter away from them.

★ ★ ★

He did not have to wait for long. Some days later, when the rain was pouring down from the heavens, a British soldier with two others beside him made it up to the door of the house silently, and knocked upon the door with a bayonet. Startled, and slow to move to the door, Bernadette called Harry, who was dozing in his chair at the head of the table.

'Harry! Someone just knocked at the door with a heavy stick or something.'

Harry took his rifle and walked to the door.

'Step back!' he shouted. 'Step back, you bastards.'

The soldiers moved a step back.

'You shits have no business here at my door. What do you want?' His voice was high-pitched and urgent.

'We were sent here by our sergeant, Major James Stapleton. We are doing our duty.'

'And what the fuck is your duty then?'

'It has become known that your daughter, Aoife O'Keeffe, was removed from the hospital in Limerick City without the consent of the hospital. The sister in charge has made a complaint to the police, and we are here to take her back to the hospital because she is a danger to herself and the community. She is not mentally sound to live outside the hospital.'

'What the fuck do they know about my daughter? If she needs anyone she has me and my wife, her mother, to look after her. She has no need to return to that despicable place.'

'Sir, we are carrying out our orders, that is all.'

'There is no fucking duty to be carried out here in this house. I will shoot the heads off you miserable fuckers. Get out of my yard as quick as you came in! Don't ever come back again to this place or I will shoot on sight, then I will string you up in the barn and skin you and throw your skin to the dog. No one will ever find you bastards.'

Slowly, they moved back while Harry stepped in line behind them until they reached the road gate.

'Fuck off now,' he shouted at them.

'We will be back.'

'It will be your last day on this earth if you come back here. I will never give up our daughter. You can be prepared to fight me, and my sons.'

The men left, to the great relief of Bernadette.

'Be careful, Harry. It's no good threatening those men; they have a job to do.'

'They will return, Ber. They won't leave a stone unturned until they get Aoife.'

They returned to the house and tried to warm themselves by the fire.

'The sister in that hospital won't be beaten; she will continue until she gets paid off or Aoife is back in there,' Harry said. 'That's what it is all about. They don't give a shit about Aoife, or any other young woman or man for that matter. All she wants is patients in her beds to keep the bishop and the local authority happy.'

'How do you know?'

'Sure, couldn't you see that for yourself?'

'I know, but they have the upper hand and can make us bring her back to that place. What can we do about it?'

'Jesus, woman, that's not going to happen. This family won't part with our daughter.'

'Maybe we should get some lawyer to take them on. I mean, they can't just take anybody they want, can they?'

'But we can't afford any lawyer.'

'Richie can.'

'More of his charity. Maybe I can make some deal where I pay in a year's time or something.'

It was no use trying to talk to Harry when he was in this kind of mood. Bernadette turned to walk away, muttering under her breath about being a charity.

'Hold on there now, woman. It's my intention to get that nursing sister or whatever she is called. I would like to pull the trigger on that bitch myself. But we will try to deal with it the legal way. I will do this myself. We won't ask Richie Fitz again; we have got enough favours from him already. He is a good person. Leave it with me now and don't start worrying about it. I'm sure they won't return here for a while anyway. I will put up a barricade and lock us in if I have to; nobody is taking Aoife from her home with us. That place is nowhere for any person to be, especially a young woman like Aoife.'

In the days that followed, Bernadette was on high alert all the time, and would jump with a fright when a neighbour would drop in to the house. But as the days went by, there was no sign of the soldiers returning to the house. What did arrive, though, was a court summons, delivered by the clerk. Mr and Mrs Harry O'Keeffe had been accused of kidnapping their own daughter, who, it alleged, had been 'removed from her hospital bed without her consent, and without the consent of the hospital and its lawful servants and administrators.'

Harry was of course furious.

'Kidnapping our own daughter? Have you ever heard of such a thing? All right, I will go to this court, and tell the whole of the county of Limerick what has happened!'

Bernadette was not so sure.

'But is Aoife going to be all right? What if they lock you up, for contempt or something? That won't help Aoife, or me!'

'I'm not going to let that happen. Anyway, we have some time yet before we need to go to court. Maybe Aoife will have the baby by that time, and then we can show the judge that she is a caring mother and well able to take care of herself and her baby.'

16.

John, the O'Keefes' elder son, was growing into a fine young man. He had girls on his mind, but was too shy to ask one of the local girls for a kiss or cuddle. He ventured over to Biddy Bergin one night after dark when morning was approaching. The door was open. Sheepishly, he entered the kitchen.

'Who is there?'

'I was hoping to talk to you.'

'Talking to me was what ye wanted, was it? Sure, there's all types. Hold on there now, mister, until I see you.'

'I'm here in your kitchen.'

'Jaysus, I know you are in my kitchen.'

Biddy emerged into the room, looking the worse for the wear.

'What is it, young O'Keeffe?'

'I want to come and visit you … just like all the men around here,' he said, sheepishly. 'No, I mean …'

'Would you not be too young for that kind of thing?'

'I am almost twenty.'

'Are there no girls your own age to do that with?'

'No, I wouldn't like to take on any of the girls around here.'

'Well now, you are a bit young for me; I might not be able for you, son. I have a lot of gentlemen callers, so to speak.'

'What harm could it do?'

'How little you know, boy. I'll tell you what, how about next Sunday morning after Mass you come straight back here after?'

'All right, I will.'

'Go on home now, young man, and let me have a sleep. I have a busy day ahead of me, between all the work here, and then the recreation at night.'

John left, and was feeling very excited about the prospect of the following Sunday. It was intoxicating. When he got home he told his brother, Brendan, about what he was going to do.

Brendan was shocked. 'Oh my God, what if Mammy and Daddy find out what you are doing? I'd say Daddy will kill you.'

'He will never know, unless you tell him.'

'Your secret is safe with me! I promise I won't tell a single person. As long as you tell me about it afterwards. Anyway, they would not believe that their favourite child would do anything like visit that auld one. What they don't know will not hurt them.'

'I am I am a man now, with a man's needs.'

'Fuck the needs; the outcome might be worse for you, Johnny.'

'It's the thrill of getting to feel the need, and then getting it. I don't care if she is ugly and old; one woman's the same as another. That's what I heard some of the men say.'

When the next Sunday arrived, John could not keep the smile off his face. Brendan was winking at him every chance he got over breakfast.

As Mass was about to begin, in Latin of course, everyone was seated, when up the centre aisle strode the bold Biddy Bergin. She stopped at the same pew as the O'Keeffes, genuflected, gravely made the sign of the cross, then slid into the seat with the O'Keeffes. The pew was full already, so they had to squeeze together to make room for her.

John felt nervous. What was this mad woman doing? Biddy had her own pew, which was paid for by her husband many years ago. It was up at the front of the altar. Why then was she sitting with them? John was uncomfortable, and felt sweat beginning to tingle on his skin. She had done this deliberately to embarrass him because he had asked her for sex.

Harry had moved along in the seat to let Biddy stay on the outside. Bernadette gave him a cut-you-in-two look. Harry grimaced back at her. Bernadette noticed that John was agitated, perspiration forming on his brow. 'Have you no hankie?' she mouthed to John. 'You are sweating. Are you sick or something?'

Trying to remain composed, John said, 'I'm all right, just a bit hot.'

He couldn't wait for Mass to end so he could get out of the church. He was unsure what Biddy was going to do. He saw his mother looking at Biddy, and John knew that his mother was quick to notice everything. He was in a panic, and was beginning to regret having made arrangements with Biddy. But he was also afraid not to keep his appointment with her in case she came looking for him. The thought of Biddy angrily turning up to their house was just too much to think about. If Harry had reacted badly to the arrival of soldiers, that was as nothing compared to what he might take it upon himself to do if Biddy Bergin arrived.

Having been instructed to go in peace to love and to serve the Lord, it was finally over. Biddy stood, but did not leave the pew, so the family had to make their way past her with all the dignity they could muster. Biddy threw an incautious wink at John, who wondered if Bernadette had seen it. What if she had? What if she knew what he planned to do? Worse, when John made his way past Biddy, their brief bodily contact presaging what was to come, she took the opportunity to pinch him on the arse. He did not flinch, but passed her by as if nothing had happened.

'Are you sure you are all right?' Bernadette said as soon as they were outside the church.

'Of course I am; why wouldn't I be?' said John, defensively, as if nothing had happened. But everybody knew that something was amiss. 'I just feel a bit hot.'

'What was that one doing sitting into our seat at Mass?' Harry remained silent.

'She can sit where she likes, can't she?'

'John, I think I saw her winking at you.'

'She was probably winking at one of the Quirkes in the pew behind us.' John was not the best at thinking quickly under pressure, but had used the time taken up by the sermon to prepare this answer, should he need it. 'She knows some of them quite well I think.'

'No doubt she does. It's a shame. Those are good Christian people; they should know better than to spend their time with the likes of that Biddy Bergin.'

'She seems to know you too, John,' said Harry, joining in the conversation for the first time.

'Not particularly,' said John. 'Strange woman.'

'Well,' said Bernadette, 'if any of ye go to her house I will get your father to give you a good hiding.'

* * *

Seanie became a household lad, and got on well with John and Brendan, who always gave him time to say what he wanted to say without sniggering and laughing. Their patience was not shared by many of the other boys who attended the dances at Byrne's, who were always sniggering and laughing at him, especially when he tried to say 'Ma and Pa' because it always came out as 'Maaah and Paaaa.' The boys would then burst into laughter, ask poor Seanie to repeat this, and then imitate it themselves.

Seanie, 'the eejit' as he was known to everyone, started calling to the O'Keeffes' home and asking after Aoife, stuttering and stammering to Bernadette that he wanted to see her. After a few days of Seanie calling, Bernadette decided to take him down to her room. Bernadette observed his eyes lighting up when he saw Aoife. He sat on the end of her bed, looking at her sheepishly and muttering. Bernadette could see a tear falling down his face. She thought, oh, poor Seanie, he is so sorry for Aoife being sick.

Seanie became a regular visitor to Aoife, spending a lot of time sitting with her in her room. He would chatter and laugh, and most of the time Aoife had no clue what he was talking about. But she knew him and liked him, and knew that he was absolutely incapable of harming her, or anybody.

Seanie had heard about what had happened to Aoife of course, and eventually worked up the courage to ask her about it. When he did, Aoife heard herself telling Seanie things that she could scarcely recall. As so often happens, Aoife learned the contents of her own mind for the first time when she heard herself saying it. The British soldiers … it all came back to her. Seanie even recognised her description of the man who had instigated the whole thing: a vicious man, he was often hanging around the barracks, and had been known to beat villagers with a stick if they so much as looked at him in the wrong way.

Aoife seemed to know everything that was going on in the home. She started dressing herself when Bernadette did. She started to help Bernadette with the jobs around the house. She went back to bed in the afternoons and rested for about two hours. She never spoke voluntarily, but answered any questions she was asked. While she was not back to herself, there was some hope now that she might make it back.

Bernadette would watch her stroking her belly and wonder if she knew what was happening to her. One day she asked, 'Aoife, do you know you are going to have a baby?'

A sharp look flashed across Aoife's normally serene face. 'A baby? What baby? I don't have any babies.'

Bernadette did not ask any more questions. There was no need to.

Richie called as usual to the O'Keeffes. He understood from them that Aoife did not know about her baby. He suggested they take her into Bruff to see the doctor. 'We must make sure she has help with the birth,' he said. 'You may need him as well as the midwife when the time comes.'

Harry had let the neighbours know of Aoife's return home, and asked them to keep it to themselves. If word got to the wrong ears they would come and take her back.

Although Aofie never went outside the door, everyone who met the O'Keeffes asked after her health. Only the family, and one or two closely trusted friends, knew that she was with child.

Arrangements needed to be made with the doctor. Richie and Bernadette would travel to Bruff. Harry said he would leave it to Bernadette to look after this.

Bruff was busy with more men than before. O'Sullivan's house was full of guests, all of them men. The place was buzzing. They kept to themselves and spoke in hushed voices. Richie knew he was not to ask any questions. So he went out walking the street. It was in darkness; there were no gas lights on the streets like back home. Yet there were people moving around everywhere. Richie had been told that his eyes would grow accustomed to the darkness, but he was yet to get used to it.

Richie waited outside the doctor's house while Bernadette and Aoife went inside to meet Doctor Oscar. A nice man, he was well known in Bruff. He had a big house with many rooms and huge windows. The front door was wide and high, with a highly polished brass knocker. When the maid opened the door they stepped inside to a huge hallway with long chandeliers hanging from the ceiling. The maid was dressed in a white starched apron over a white skirt. Her hair was black and curly. She was very efficient, greeting the two women and asking them to come in.

The house smelled sterile with not a thing out of place. Bernadette couldn't get over the grandeur of the place. The doctor sat behind a very fancy desk. He had a gentle smile on his face.

'Sit down, ladies,' he said, gesturing to the chairs in front of his desk. 'What can I do for you today?'

'If you could work a miracle?' Bernadette said with a humourless chuckle.

'The impossible I can do now; a miracle will take a little longer.' He grinned a grin that had reassured many of Bruff's inhabitants over the years.

Bernadette explained the situation regarding the pregnancy. As she did so, his face reddened somewhat, perhaps embarrassed by his earlier air of optimism and calm.

'I see. I see. She is young to be having children. You poor girl,' he said, addressing Aoife directly. 'This is not the first time mothers have come here with their daughters like this. You'll be fine. Lie down over here and let me have a look at you.'

Aoife tentatively made her way over to the raised bed. As the doctor began to place his hands upon her swollen belly she became intensely uncomfortable, breaking out in a sweat. Before long she was shouting and screaming, terrified. Bernadette tried to console her, but nothing she could say had the effect of calming Aoife down.

'It's all right,' Oscar said. 'We won't do anything to you.'

Aoife's eyes darted to the doorway, and moments later she made a run for it, only to find the door locked. She screamed once more, and then fell to the floor, sobbing.

'Perhaps Aoife would be better off giving birth at home?' Oscar said. 'The poor girl is terrified, aren't you?' He took hold of her hand. 'I think you might be better off in your own home with your family around you to care for you.'

He turned to Bernadette.

'There is a midwife living near Loch Gurr. I think it best that you call on her. These situations are not uncommon, Mrs O'Keeffe. She might be able to call on you at home when the time comes.'

'Thank you, doctor.'

'You might not know it, but there could be consequences for me if I were to attend the birth myself.'

'But if anything were to go wrong....'

'I am sure that all will be fine. Honestly, Aoife needs to be as relaxed as possible, and clearly being at home would be much more conducive to that.'

Oscar unlocked the door. Bernadette helped Aoife to her feet.

'Thank you, doctor.'

The maid showed them out. Bernadette was unsure whether she was being fobbed off or whether Oscar might really face some difficulties of his own with the British Crown. She knew little enough about such matters. But he was clearly right that Aoife needed to remain in her own home rather than upsetting herself any further.

The maid showed them out the door.

'Sorry for your trouble, ma'am,' she said. 'The doctor cannot be seen to deliver babies of unmarried mothers, you see.'

Bernadette just nodded her head resignedly and left with her daughter, both of them distraught.

★ ★ ★

On the following day, Richie drove them out to Loch Gurr to visit the midwife who had been recommended to them. They had no difficulty in finding her. People would take one look at Aoife and simply point in the direction they needed.

She proved to be friendly, if informal.

'And how many months is she gone?'

'Well I'm not sure,' she replied. You see....'

Bernadette petered out.

'I understand. I can come out to you and help. Perhaps I should call over tomorrow, if that is convenient. Then we can make more arrangements for when the little one is ready to arrive.'

Bernadette was relieved to have the midwife on board.

She proved to be as good as her word, and called to the O'Keeffes' house the very next day. She was kind to Aoife, explaining to her how things would go when the baby arrived. Aoife remained in a dreamlike state.

'Do you understand?'

Aoife did not reply. The midwife looked at Bernadette, concerned.

'I won't be available to deliver. I am so sorry. I don't know what you are going to do, Mrs O'Keeffe, but Aoife is

not responding to me at all. I can see she does not understand what I am saying to her. That's the reason I cannot
help her.'

She left without suggesting anything.

Harry, who was outside and had seen her leaving, came
into the room asking what the midwife had to say.

'She cannot come to help either.'

'What the fuck is going on? The Doctor can't help,
now the midwife can't help?'

'What are we going to do now?'

'I will ask old Mrs Buckley. I know she delivered all her
own children without any help from anyone. Maybe she
will come and help you too.'

Bernadette did not reply. She was more than nervous
that things could go wrong, and then what would they do?

'What's the worst thing could happen?' Harry asked.

'Well, the baby could die, or they both could die. It
could be a very long labour as this is her first child. And
probably her only one.'

Mrs Buckley was happy to help with the delivery of
Aoife's baby. It was a lifeline of sorts.

'I had so many myself,' she said, laughing, 'I can hardly
count them! The older children had gone to America
before the younger ones were born, so they don't know
one another at all. If they met on the street they would
walk by one another. I am finished having children I hope.
Sure I have four grandchildren in America whom I will
never see as it is. They are all good to write to me and send
money when they can. You get everything prepared. I know
it's not due yet, but there's no harm in having everything in
place before the labour begins. We will have enough to do
without having to go into town to buy things.'

Aoife was not engaging in any conversation, just staring blankly into the space ahead of her. Mrs Buckley was

not fazed by this; she was clearly one of those people who believe that everything would invariably fall into place when the time came.

'It is always best to deliver a baby naturally in your own place I think. It will be up to us to see that both mother and baby are safe.'

When Bernadette heard Mrs Buckley say 'mother and baby', she felt the emotions welling up inside her. Somehow it affected her more this time, talking with her neighbour, than it did with any other person talking about the baby.

The reality had taken over. Sometimes a good-natured neighbour could be one of the most important blessings of life. With or without this kindness and help, though, the fact was that a woman who was pregnant out of wedlock was sure to be shunned by the community. Aoife's future was to be whispered about, called a slut, and thought of as a fallen woman to be avoided. If she ended up at the mother and baby home, she could expect to work hard from early in the morning until late at night, right up until the point when her labour began. When the baby arrived it would be taken from her and looked after by nuns until it was put up for adoption. That none of this was Aoife's fault would count for little in this place at this time. All that would matter was that the family would be disgraced. The O'Keeffes saw all of this, but could do little to avoid it.

★ ★ ★

On some of Seanie's visits to the O'Keeffes he began a relationship with Aoife's two brothers. He was friendlier with Brendan, being about the same age. Brendan would chat with him about the Irish Republican Brotherhood, about which Seanie knew little. It was young Brendan's intention, unbeknownst to his parents, to join up. He admired the men, and was very taken with their effort to take back Ireland from the British. He spoke to Seanie and explained what they were about. Seanie wanted to join as well, and got excited about the notion. Here was something that even Seanie had no difficulty understanding. He wanted to know what he could do to help and be beside Brendan on the job. Brendan suggested that they both go to the next meeting at O'Sullivan's bar in the town of Bruff. Seanie couldn't wait. Brendan swore him to secrecy, warning him that the whole thing would fall apart if he gave the game away.

The meeting was to take place the next week on a Monday night, where they would enlist any recruits who would come forward. All the week, Seanie was so excited he could hardly sit for a few moments at a time. His parents wanted to find out what was so exciting. They asked him many times to tell them, but he managed to remember what Brendan had said and resolutely refused to open his mouth.

When the night came for them to go into Bruff, they set out on the road hours before the meeting. Brendan was trying to convince Seanie that he needed to calm down or they would not get the chance to join anything. They waited outside Sullivan's, expecting to see someone entering the bar, but nobody did. After another hour or so, Brendan decided to enter. Sullivan was behind the bar. 'Well, lads, what can I do for you?'

Brendan moved forwards and whispered, 'We are here to join. But we can't see anyone coming or going. We don't know what to do.'

'Go to the back yard and through the big door in front of you; that's where they are. Are ye sure that's what you want to do? Are ye too young?'

Brendan assured him that they were both over eighteen years old. With that, Sullivan gave up and returned to his business.

When they opened the door, all they could see was a fog of tobacco smoke. When their eyes had acclimatised to it they could make out the men who had fallen silent and now stared at the two of them. 'Who are you?' the man in charge demanded.

Brendan took off his cap and said, gravely, 'We are here to join up with you. We want to serve our country.'

'Come and take a seat, then.' He gestured towards the wooden bench to the side of the shed. 'Well, boys, what experience do you have?'

'… none,' replied Brendan, ashamed.

'No practice with guns?'

'No.'

'So you have no experience of anything?'

'It affects us as much as anybody. We want to help.'

'Can ye work at night covering for your companions?'

'Yes, sir, we can.'

He turned to Seanie. 'And what about you?'

Seanie looked at Brendan, who shoved him in the ribs. Still, Seanie stood silently.

'What's the matter with you?'

'He has a stammer, sir, and doesn't talk very well. But there is nothing wrong with him. I have known him all my life.'

'He looks like a fucking eejit to me.'

'He is good at keeping things to himself; he won't tell anyone anything.'

'I suppose that is true.'

There was laughter around the shed. Even Seanie joined in. The two of them took an oath that evening to the other members of the Brotherhood to take back their country. Brendan and Seanie had made a big decision, and both of them knew it. On the walk home, the two were nervous. Seanie was certain that they had done the right thing. Brendan was more concerned about what was going to happen. 'Just keep your mouth shut, Seanie. About everything, you understand? Just keep your mouth shut and we will be all right.'

★ ★ ★

John O'Keeffe walked up to Biddy Bergin's door, which was open. He knocked anyway. 'Is that you, John? Come in, won't you?'

John, trying to remain calm, made his way through the door. He was trying to keep calm. As Biddy Bergin led him through to her bedroom and onto the bed, John could feel himself becoming hard. Biddy saw this and grinned. 'You don't waste much time, do you?'

'What? I ...'

'Come here, boy, and I'll make you a man. That's what you want, isn't it?'

'I ... yes ... I ...'

Her practised hands deftly removed his trousers, hitched up her skirt, and then led his stiff cock to exactly where it needed to go. He slid into her, and moments later John came, shouting and moaning with pleasure and excitement.

'That was ... great.'

'You will enjoy it more when you learn to take your time. That comes with practice.'

'Practice? I see the bull in the field, and he has it done in a flash. There is no taking time, it's just go at it and get it done.'

'Well you did that all right.' She smiled, and giggled a little. 'You will understand after a while.'

Biddy could feel John growing hard inside her once again.

'Even for one so young, it usually takes a bit longer than that.'

She rolled on top of him, rocking backwards and forwards gently. John knew, of course, that he had discovered the secret of the world. This was what he wanted to do, this and nothing else, all of the time. He pulled her dress down roughly. His hands were on her breasts, and then her arse, and then everywhere at once. John could contain himself no longer, and came a second time, this time deep inside Biddy, who was panting as well. She groaned deeply as she rolled off him to his side.

'That was much better already, lad.'

When John returned home, guilt was written all over his face, where it competed with a wide grin. Bernadette took one look at him and asked, 'Where were you, John? Were you talking to a girl by any chance? I saw Kathleen Maguire gazing at you coming down from Holy Communion. Are you interested in her? She is a fine girl for her age.'

'No, Mother, I am not interested in Kathleen Maguire at all. She has a boyfriend already and it's not me.'

'Are they any girls you admire at Mass?'

'No, not one of them.'

'Where did you go today?'

'Nowhere. I took my time checking the cattle, that's all. Stop questioning me, Mother; I am doing nothing wrong.'

'I donk know about that now, Johnny boy. Don't go getting some girl in the family way, now do you hear that?'

John went to his bedroom to change his clothes. He could smell Biddy on him. Maybe his mother could too. He didn't care. He had discovered the secret of the world: the greatest pleasure to which a man could aspire was to be found between a woman's legs. Nothing else could ever come close to that feeling. How could it? This was everything that mattered. This was what made people write poetry and music. John could think of nothing else. All he wanted was to get back over to Biddy Bergin's house, and to get inside her once again. Who knew how much there was for him to learn and enjoy? His mother was probably jealous, he reflected. What did she know?

17.

Richie was content with the fact that Aoife would have someone to help with the delivery, although he was shocked at the doctor's, and the midwife's, refusal to help. What were these people for if not to help somebody in Bernadette's situation? He could not begin to imagine. They were a law unto themselves, and it was not right. At least they had Mrs Buckley's help.

Harry O'Keeffe found it hard not to notice his daughter's increasing size. He told Bernadette that he hoped the baby would arrive soon. It saddened him greatly; he had had enough of looking at his wife sitting by the fire every night and knitting. She finished one garment; she started another. 'I must make some clothes for the baby. What would we do if the baby came and we had no clothes for to keep it warm?' she had said. But it was turning into an obsession. She had knitted and crocheted blankets, matinee coats and a few other baby things. They were stacked in a box near the fire to keep them aired and at the ready.

'Everything will come in good time,' said Bernadette.

'Is there any way we can hurry this on and get back to some normality?' asked Harry, somewhat defeated by the situation.

'Of course not,' replied Bernadette. She was cross. 'We can't hurry anything; you know that. It will come when it's ready and not before.'

Harry talked as best he could about their financial situation. Things were becoming serious, and he felt ashamed in front of his neighbours. The thought of what they might consider to be his reduced circumstances upset him at least as much as those circumstances themselves.

'I was the one giving advice; now I'm the one in trouble. I can't stand it any more.'

Bernadette knew how her husband was feeling. He was proud and a good-living man.

'There is nothing we can do about the situation, only make the best of it now. Whatever happens we must stick together as a family. It's all we have at the end of the day.'

Harry walked away, his head bowed.

Bernadette noticed that Aoife was unsettled. She did not say a lot, and did not complain. But she would sit and get up, walk around with her hands stroking her belly, then lie down again. She went to bed early, and was asleep when Bernadette came into the room to join her. She was relieved to see Aoife asleep. In truth, it was a relief to Bernadette to see her daughter still, asleep, looking peaceful in a way that she rarely did in her waking hours.

When Bernadette had her head on the pillow, though, Aoife sat up in the bed. She shrieked, holding her belly. As fast as she could, Bernadette called Harry.

'Get down to Mrs Buckley as fast as you can. I think Aoife is in labour.'

Harry ran.

Before Mrs Buckley came to the house, Aoife's water had broken. She was in shock, and barely understood what was happening to her.

Bernadette was quick to console her and reassure her that she was fine and well able to deliver her baby. She had stoked the fire and put the heavy pots of water on ready for the baby to come.

Aoife fell asleep again just for a few seconds, before waking again with a screech. Mrs Buckley and Harry were coming in the kitchen door when there was another screech. Mrs Buckley went white in the face. 'Oh, the poor child, she is in agony. The sooner she delivers, the better.'

They entered the bedroom, where Aoife was doubled up in pain.

'Take your time; the baby will come when it's ready.'

Aoife began to push and push, with more fluid coming. Mrs Buckley could begin to see the baby's head.

'Relax,' she advised Aoife. 'It only makes it worse if you are all tensed up. It won't be long now at all.'

But it was. It went on for another three hours until Aoife was exhausted and ready to give up.

'Just one more big push, and as hard as you can.'

The baby's head was out. Mrs Buckley caught hold of it with the next contraction.

'Push as hard and as long as you can.'

She did, and out came a baby girl, already with a head of red hair. She put the baby up on Aoife's chest, waiting for some reaction. Nothing happened; she just looked stunned. Then the little baby began to cry. Aoife put her hand on the baby's head, stroking it gently, and said, 'Shush now, little one.'

'You have a beautiful healthy baby girl,' Mrs Buckley said.

A big smile came across her face.

'Is this mine?' Aoife asked Bernadette, who was in floods of tears at this stage.

'Yes,' she said. 'This little angel is yours.'

She laid her head back on the pillow and took a deep sigh.

'That was so hard,' Aoife muttered. She rocked the baby in her arms and took her to her breast.

'That's nature,' Mrs Buckley said. 'Everything is going to be fine now she has taken to the baby.'

The two women cleaned up Aoife and the baby, dressed the little thing and put her into the bed beside her mother. Harry knocked on the door.

'What's happening? Has the baby arrived yet?'

'Yes,' said Bernadette, opening the door, 'we have a baby girl, the sweetest little thing ever.'

'How is Aoife?'

Harry remained outside the door, not wanting to go into the room.

'She is exhausted, but she's fine.'

Mrs Buckley moved over to Harry.

'She is young and well able to bring a child into the world. Come and see your daughter and your new granddaughter.'

'I won't. I ... I can't.'

Harry was not excited by the birth. All he could think of was that awful day when Aoife came up the lane, broken into pieces. He was angry about what had happened to his daughter, and the new baby only served to remind him of it.

Bernadette was like a second mother, fussing over everything. She saw that her husband was not himself, and was concerned that he would not take to the baby.

When Mrs Buckley left the next morning, Bernadette was alone with Aoife. She did not want to leave her side. There was no breakfast cooked and no dinner that evening

— only tea and bread was served in the O'Keeffe household.

'Are we all to starve on account of a new baby?' Harry asked.

Bernadette ignored him. She was in a different space entirely. Seeing Aoife mothering the new baby brought joy to her heart of a kind that she had not known for many years.

Bernadette was hoping that Richie would call to see the baby and how Aoife was doing. Sure enough, he turned up the following day. He couldn't believe the baby had arrived and that child and mother were both doing well.

'It's a little girl,' Bernadette told him. 'Aoife has taken to her with no problem at all. Come on down to the room and see for yourself.'

Richie followed Bernadette, only to find Aoife sitting out of the bed with the baby in her arms.

'Hello, Aoife. I have come to see your new baby.'

There was no reply from Aoife. Bernadette moved in to take the baby and let Richie hold it. Aoife reacted violently, shouting and waving her free arm. She did not want her mother to take her baby.

'Aoife, I won't take your baby; I have just come to visit with the family.'

It was only then Bernadette saw there was going to be a problem. Richie had never seen a newborn before.

'What lovely hair she has,' Richie said. 'Already with hair! And what lovely little fingers. You're perfect, aren't you.' He played with the baby's tiny hands. 'She is fine and healthy,' he said.

Bernadette told Richie how Mrs Buckley had come at a minute's notice and how good she was with the delivery, although Aoife had to do all the work herself bringing the baby into the world.

Aoife's two brothers showed no interest at all in the new baby; they were embarrassed that their sister had a baby and was not married. Yet they were intrigued, watching the little baby move and smile.

'She smiles when she's playing with the angels, don't you?' Bernadette said to Richie. 'I remember when Aoife was a baby too. She was so quiet. My first son was the hardest; he was a big baby, maybe ten pounds. I thought he was never going to come out. When he finally decided to arrive, he was in a big hurry! But he was no bother; all he wanted was feeding and sleeping.'

'I'm sure you never forget having babies,' Richie said, 'especially your firstborn.'

When Richie congratulated Harry on the arrival of his granddaughter, all he got was a grunt. 'I only wish my girl had been married,' Harry said beneath his breath.

Richie knew not to comment any more.

★ ★ ★

For the next two weeks Aoife stayed in her room, not letting the baby out of her sight. Bernadette did everything she could to entice her out of the room and down to the kitchen for her meals, which she had gradually resumed cooking, but Aoife wanted to stay there with the baby. Bernadette took her meals to her in the room. She did the washing for her and the baby. She spent most of her time taking care of them. Harry complained; the disruption in the home meant that his dinner was not on the table at the usual times of day.

Bernadette was not impressed by these complaints.

'Would you go 'way outta that?' she said. 'I have a more important job to do looking after our daughter and our grandchild.'

'Grandchild? What grandchild are you talking about, woman? That child belongs to someone else and does not belong to us.'

'Are you mad or what? Of course she belongs to us! Our daughter gave birth to this little baby. She is our granddaughter.'

'Well I don't see it like that.' He walked off out to the yard, pausing to shout behind him, 'What time will we get dinner around here?'

'Come when I call you,' Bernadette said.

Harry was uneasy in himself. It seemed he did not get Bernadette's attention in the manner to which he had become accustomed. Aoife's baby was taking up all of Bernadette's time. She was finding it hard to cope with everything, but did not let it be known to the family, or to Richie.

At long last, Aoife dressed herself and the baby and came down to the kitchen, where she sat on her father's chair with the little baby in her arms. The red hair was starting to curl up behind her head. She looked brighter, and the baby looked fine and healthy.

Bernadette suggested that it was time to christen the baby and make her a child of God.

'Have you thought about a name for the baby, Aoife?' Bernadette asked.

Aoife looked straight ahead, and then replied to her mother.

'She is a baby, so I will call her "Babba".'

'No,' said Bernadette, 'we need to give her a proper name. Would you name her after yourself?'

'No, then we would have two Aoifes. I wouldn't like that at all,' she said.

Leaving the subject to go and cook dinner, Bernadette turned and said, 'What about "Eileen"? Would you like that?'

Aoife did not reply.

'I want to name her "Gertrude"; something is telling me she is Gertrude.

'I like that name,' Bernadette said. 'It sounds good with the name O'Keeffe. We will have a little Gertrude O'Keeffe.'

As those words were spoken, a huge gust of wind opened the kitchen door. It swept through the kitchen, sending ashes from the grate and leaving dust everywhere, it came down the chimney too, and covered Aoife and the baby with soot from the chimney. It scared the two women; Bernadette ran to Aoife and brushed her down. Although the soot had lodged in the baby's eyes, she did not make a sound, but Aoife was upset. She worried about the baby.

'She's all black. That soot could kill her, mammy,' she said.

Bernadette got a basin of warm water and gave the baby a nice bath. She washed Aoife's hair too. While busy cleaning up the kitchen she had no time to think about the gust of wind. It had happened a few times before. She waited until that night when everyone was gone to bed to tell Harry. Harry could not explain why this was happening.

'We will have to find out what is causing this. I don't know what to do about it.'

Harry could not think of anyone who could help them find out what was happening. As Aoife and her baby settled into a routine, Bernadette got back to cooking dinner and looking after the boys.

Richie called once or twice a week to visit and check how things were going with the family. There were some more gusts of wind when Aoife was in the kitchen with her baby, Gertrude. One evening Aoife was settling the baby down for the night; she had the little baby at her breast, feeding. The wind came again; this time it almost knocked the baby out of her mother's arms. This unsettled Aoife. She looked to her mother for some explanation.

'What is happening in this house? The wind almost knocked the baby out of my arms. It's always happening now,' she said to her mother.

Bernadette knew that the wind had got more frequent since the baby arrived in the house. She could not understand it either. Although she had asked Harry, he knew no more than she did about it, except that something was causing the spirit to get angry again. It happened when Richie Fitzgerald came to the house for the first time.

'Now that the baby is here I think the spirit wants to dwell in the baby.'

This frightened Bernadette, who couldn't believe this could happen.

She had noticed when Aoife named the baby Gertrude the gust of wind came then.

'It's better to have her christened now. Maybe that will console the spirit or protect the little thing.'

They made arrangements with the priest to take the baby to Mass the next Sunday and do the christening before Mass. There was another woman with a baby there to be christened too, but Aoife's little girl was first. He christened her, 'Gertrude, in the name of the Father the Son and the Holy Spirit.' He made the sign of the cross on the child and poured holy water over her head as the baby looked around at the priest and at her mother. She looked scared, but did not cry.

After Mass, the parents of the baptised babies went into the presbytery to make an official record.

'Father's name?' the priest asked.

'No father,' replied Harry.

The priest looked Aoife over.

'Do you not know who the father is?

'No one,' said Aoife, speaking for herself. 'It is like Holy Mary the mother of God; she got pregnant and she had no man or husband. This happened to me too.'

The priest just went along to the next parents. Bernadette was heartbroken for her daughter.

Before they left the presbytery, the priest gave them a certificate of baptism. Harry shoved it into his breast pocket and asked the women to come on home now. The priest called them back for a quiet moment between them. Looking at Aoife, he said, 'You are naming your baby after the little girl who lived in that house before she went out foreign. She too was Gertrude. Her father called her Trudy. Will you shorten it to Trudy?'

'I don't know,' Aoife said. 'It keeps coming into my head about that name. It's like someone is whispering it in my ear. "Her name is Gertrude, her name is Gertrude". That's why I named her that name. But I like that name anyway.'

Harry walked out of the presbytery, putting his hat on as he did so.

'We must be off home now,' he said to his two women.

Richie Fitzgerald was waiting for them outside. He was beaming with a smile.

'How are all my family?'

'We are happy to have little Gertrude christened; she is a child of God now,' said Bernadette.

Harry headed for the pony and trap while Richie offered to take the women home in his car. They were delighted to take him up on his offer.

'So, she's christened now.'

'She is. Gertrude,' said Bernadette.

'She looks so peaceful since she has her own name,' added Aoife.

'Ah no,' said Bernadette. 'It's because she is God's child now.'

She remembered her mother saying that when the babies are christened they settle down, sleep all night and are more content in themselves.

'She is happy, anyway,' Aoife reminded her mother.

Seanie was too taken up with the Brotherhood to come every day to sit with Aoife. They had given him and Brendan each a large a canvas bag to hide in the barn, and Seanie fussed over his endlessly, checking that it had not been discovered or disturbed. This bag had to be kept safe and dry, and needed to be ready at a moment's notice.

Whilst Seanie was delighted with this new responsibility, Brendan was not nearly so content with these 'duties', and wanted to be involved in more exciting activities. He wanted to practice shooting and to be a good marksman. How else could he kill their enemies and free Ireland? He was concerned that Seanie would let the cat out of the bag about their membership of the Brotherhood. Why had he brought Seanie with him? It had seemed like a good idea at the time, but now he was not so sure.

The two of them decided that they would assign themselves additional responsibilities, and took it upon themselves to patrol the village in secret, looking out for anything out of the ordinary that might be of importance to the Brotherhood and its operations. Being the young men they were, they took particular pleasure in investigating

Biddy Bergin's house in the early hours, which often proved to be educational as well as exciting.

Until, on one of these clandestine patrols, they found her motionless. She was dead.

They could not report their discovery without needing to answer questions about what they had been doing at Biddy Bergin's cottage in the early hours of the morning, and so they decided to say nothing and let nature take its course.

Three other gentlemen callers learned in similar circumstances that Biddy Bergin was not available to them that night, and each made the same decision.

And so it was the postman who officially 'found' her the next morning when he came to deliver letters. Even though the local women had no time for Biddy, who was the cause of more inter marital arguments than unpaid bills, few were now willing to speak ill of the dead

Friends and neighbours paid their respects. Many of Bruff's menfolk owed something to Biddy, not least of them John O'Keeffe, who missed her especially keenly. The usual prayers with candlelight were said at night. The doctor gave a decision that she had died of natural causes.

She was buried beside her husband. The headstone reads: 'Here lies John Bergin and his beloved and devoted wife Bridget (Biddy).'

More than a few of the married ladies of Bruff soon realised that what their husbands would not find in one place they would find in another. After their satisfied men had eventually fallen asleep, they would reflect upon the truth that Biddy Bergin had not been an entirely negative influence upon their lives. Biddy had allowed the women to feel morally and spiritually superior, whilst allowing the men to feel potent and daring. Some of the men of Bruff now expected their wives to provide them with all of the services that Biddy had offered, and not all of the wives were enamoured of this. This 'outsider' did much to cement the group together, and now that she was gone, things would change.

The women needed Biddy Bergin even more than their men did.

18.

When Richie got back to Bruff that evening he decided to tackle the bundle of letters. One by one he laid them out on the bed, checking the postmark and date on them. He sorted them into order, and began with the oldest one. The letter and envelope were light in his hand; the writing was in heavy black ink. It was addressed to Richard Fitzgerald, from Trudy in South Africa. As he read down the page, he could feel her concern for her father.

Daddy, I have not heard from you for such a long time. I am worried about you. Are you taking care of yourself? I hope you are eating good food, and going to the doctor about your bad cough. When I don't hear from you I worry, so please reply to my letters—it will only take you a few minutes. I think of you at home on your own, and no one to make a cup of tea for you. I wish you would make the journey to South Africa and live with me. The weather is always good, but a little too hot at times. It would suit you with all the pains and aches you have. It would be just grand to have you here with me? My staff would look after you. You would live like a high king.

Everything is going well here. The hotel is better than I ever thought business is very good on account of the gold mines and all the work that comes with that.

No, I never married, and I'm sure I won't at this stage. I am probably happier on my own, and am content with my own company. I have family all around me with the staff I have. I want for nothing.

How are things with the neighbours? Do you hear from my older brothers in Boston?

Hoping to hear from you.

Your loving daughter,

Trudy

Richie felt sad to think that her father never got the letter, and Trudy never got a reply.

The next one, brown, had a British postmark. The heading of the letter showed the British crown.

Richard Fitzgerald,

Your land entitlements have ceased. You have one month from the date of this letter to leave the house and surrounding lands.

It was not easy to read. That poor man. At least he never received this particular letter. Anybody treated in that way might become a recluse and keep a gun close at hand, Richie reflected. It could drive anybody mad.

The next letter had a symbol in red wax across the sealed part of the envelope. He had to break the seal to open the letter. It felt bulky. As he opened it he could see it was banknotes. There was £200 in total from the two sons in Boston. A note accompanied the money:

Father,

We hope you are well and still in our home. We heard many of our neighbours were moved out and live on the side of the road now. We don't want this to happen to you. Pay the landlord with this and keep them off your back for a while.

We are doing well over here. The work is hard, but we are well used to it now. We have a good life with our wives and family. If you would like to, come and live with us—we would be very delighted. It's no good on your own, trying to keep everything going.

Let us know when you receive this letter.

Richie didn't know what to do about this letter and the money it contained. It was useless to Aunt Trudy; she didn't need it, and couldn't spend it anyway.

He had never known the men in Boston; they were probably dead and well gone by this time. The girl who could do with some financial help that he knew was Aoife O'Keeffe. This money could be a great help to her and her baby. She had never had money at any time in her life, and this could help to bring her some happiness, clothes for her baby, and a cot with some blankets.

He walked down the street to Flynn's drapery and haberdasher's shop. He handed the lady behind the counter a list of things he would pick up the next morning. The shop assistant looked surprised when she checked the list. Everyone she came in contact with was surprised too. The shop assistant's account of the items required went around the locality like wildfire. She quoted the list to many.

1. A baby cot and pram
2. Blankets and sheets for the cot and the pram
3. Baby clothes, five sets of everything
4. Towel napkins
5. Anything else you may think that a new baby will require

She had to take the list to her boss; it was the longest list of things that she had ever been given.

'Is it the yank who is staying down at O'Sullivan's lodging house?'

'Yes, sir, that is the man.'

'Do we have everything on the list that he wants? You can pack up everything except the cot and the pram, which we will leave ready for collection at the shop's front door.'

'Yes, sir.'

'And who is having a new baby? News of these things rarely escapes my wife.'

'I don't know, sir. No one knows.'

Richie picked up his order from Flynn's early the next morning, paying in full for everything.

It was a very good year for Flynn's.

The women of Bruff were not known for their respect for the privacy of others, and there was much speculation regarding who the items were for. They even asked the doctor's secretary, Nellie, who was having a baby soon, but Nellie, for once, did not have the answer.

Richie met Harry in the lane. He stopped the car.

'I brought some things for the baby. I don't know if they are the right things, really, but I thought I would try to help.'

'I don't know anything about things for babies; Bernadette is the one for all that kind of thing. I was never involved in women's stuff.'

Richie looked surprised. Harry, not much given to introspection, caught a brief glance of himself through Richie's eyes.

'Us men have more to do then sorting out things for new babies; it's the woman of the house's job to look after these things.'

He nodded agreement with himself.

'Well it's time she had everything she needs for her baby.'

He made his way to the house proper, extracting the pram from the car and rolling it up over the doorstep and into the house. Bernadette and Aoife came out to see who was coming. When they saw Richie, a shock of delight came over their faces.

'What is it?' Aoife asked.

'It's for your baby, Gertrude, to lie in while you take her for a walk down the country roads.'

'I have never seen one of these. How does it work?' It turned out that Aoife's question regarding who the pram was for was not entirely redundant after all — she had never seen such a thing before.

Richie explained while Bernadette nodded her head in agreement. Bernadette had seen a pram before, although she had never owned one.

'Well, this is the first pram to ever cross the threshold,' she said to Richie.

'I am so delighted to give it to you. I have more things in the car for you — everything a new baby needs!'

Except a father, thought Harry, but he kept his opinion to himself.

Excitement came over the two women as they opened the parcel of baby clothes. Richie helped them to get the new cot to Aoife's bedroom. He had to explain to Aoife, 'This is a bed for your baby to sleep in.' She wasn't used to such a thing. Once the blankets and sheets were arranged in the cot, Aoife placed her baby in it. She stood back to have a good look. For the first time in a long time, a huge smile played across her face.

'I don't know how to thank you. You didn't need to do all of this for me. All these things … these things you have brought me … the baby will be safe in the cot, and I can walk over to the neighbours' with Gertrude in the pram.'

★ ★ ★

Outside in the yard, Harry was washing the milk churns, getting them ready for the evening's milking.

'You're a great man, Richie,' he said. 'Sometimes I am too proud. It isn't easy to ask for a bit of help, you know? Anyway, thank you. Thank you.'

He clapped Richie on the back.

'Any time, Harry. What is money for if you can't do some good with it? In fact, there is a bit left over, and I would like you to take it.'

'I can't take that from you,' Harry said. 'Jesus, but you've done enough for us already.'

'Well, it's not mine, not like I earned it anyway, so you take it and pay some of your debts with it.'

'But how will I ever repay you?'

'There is no need, Harry. I told you: how can a friend be in debt? I have more than I need already. Come on, now; you'll hurt my feelings if you refuse.'

Harry put the bank notes wrapped in brown paper into his trouser pocket and kept on working.

'Stay for dinner? Although it could take a while; the women are so busy with the baby it's hard to get a bit of grub around here these times. Bernadette will have your name in the pot anyway.'

'I can't. I am heading across to Brannigan's to enquire about Mr Brannigan senior; he has not been well these last few weeks.'

'Really?'

'Yeah. They think he had pneumonia. He is bad with it.'

The two men headed off down the lane and out onto the road. The sky above them got heavy with black clouds. Harry slowed down.

'The heavens are going to open in a few minutes.'

With that, there was a clap of thunder, quickly followed by a downpour of rain. Harry and Richie stood under a huge oak tree at the side of the road. They were close together. Harry produced a pouch of tobacco from inside his coat and began to fill his pipe.

'How are you, Harry?' Richie asked.

Harry cast his eyes towards the ground.

'It has been all I can do just to make ends meet, Richie. You have been great, really. I don't know what we would have done. The landlord is on our back for the rent. They want to evict us. After all the years and all the work here, evicted.' He shook his head. 'Bernadette doesn't know quite how bad things have become. Things have been going downhill, but sure I try and keep the worry away from them.'

'What will happen if you do get evicted?'

'The same that happens to any other family: we will have to walk out of the house, *their* house but *our* home, and live by the side of the fuckin' road.'

Richie was shocked. As the rain beat down around them, he felt the hardness of the land. This was not an easy place to live in; it was a constant struggle.

'And what you will live on?'

'Fresh air! I wish I knew. It will be the end of us as a family. It makes a man feel like he has failed. I don't think I deserved that. I'm thinking of sending the two lads off to America or Canada. I believe Australia is looking for people to come and work there. The convicts are sent there, and I hear they have a good living. The fucking convicts over there do better than we do here! The boys are old enough to go and work in another country, and that is probably what they should do. As for Aoife, she will never marry now with the baby. No man will want her. So in the end, it will be the four of us. I feel we are too old to go to another land and live there. I am well able for work, but I don't think Bernadette would settle in another country.'

He smoked his pipe. Richie knew that he was looking at a broken man.

'You are in an awful predicament indeed. I hope that things change for you. God knows, you deserve it.'

The rain stopped, and the men walked on.

'Our conversation is just between us, you understand?'

'Of course, Harry.' There was a pause as the wind whistled around them. 'I hope that woman the banshee is not coming around here yet.'

A single look from Harry told Richie that he did not consider it to be a laughing matter.

When they arrived at Brannigan's, Mr Brannigan senior was in the parlour, lying in his bed, a white crocheted bedspread over him and a crisp, white pillow under his head. He seemed to be sleeping gently. Both men sat beside the bed silently. Harry was praying, his lips moving but the sound inaudible. Then he put the sign of the cross on himself, stood, and dipped his fingers into a bowl of holy water beside the bed, putting the sign of the cross on Mr Brannigan's forehead.

There were many more neighbours coming into the house. Some carrying a basket of food or other token. The neighbouring women had made tea and sandwiches with ham and cheese, which most other neighbours devoured.

Harry and Richie went on their way home with no delay.

19.

*B*ack at the O'Keeffes' home, Richie stayed for dinner. He was happy looking at Aoife and her baby.

A gust of wind came and went, the door opening and closing, and whistling down the chimney. Harry got up from the table and got the holy water and started flicking it around the kitchen. He blessed everyone with it, and the baby too. All was quiet for a moment. When the baby cried, gusts of wind from outside somehow answered.

Harry and Bernadette looked shaken.

'What is that?' Richie asked.

'We don't know,' Harry replied. 'But it's happening more and more since the baby arrived.'

Aoife butted in, 'It's not the baby's fault; she didn't do anything wrong.'

'Ah, no,' Harry said, 'it's nothing the baby did; it's the spirit in the house is angry with the little one. All we can do is pray for the lost soul that's left behind here. It doesn't like the holy water I just spread around the place! I wonder why that is? It can't be the devil; he had no part in our lives.'

'Maybe that's just it,' Bernadette said. 'We won't do the holy water again when the wind comes. We will ask it what it wants.'

'Sure, for God's sake, woman, do you think that the spirit is going to answer you?'

Richie said nothing, but found it hard to understand why there was any need for supernatural explanations. The only forces of evil that had truly harmed the O'Keefes had been in very human form. If there was any kind of spirit in the house, perhaps it did not like him being there. Maybe it was all just superstition, but on his first night in the house he had felt distinctly uncomfortable. Something about the oldness of the place brought it out in him.

'Mostly spirits who dwell in old houses like ours are there for many generations back,' said Harry, gravely. 'I have heard about this before, but I thought all this kind of thing was long gone and didn't happen any more. But now I wonder if something has disturbed a spirit, and it's angry. I don't know how to make it peaceful.'

'But what have we done to offend some spirit?' said Bernadette?

'Maybe it is my presence here,' Richie said. 'Like I am not supposed to be here, or something?'

'Who knows?'

Harry reflected on what had happened.

'There had been these gusts of wind through the house ever since you got here. Sure, wind like that might blow hot embers from the fire grate into the house and set fire to it.' It had never bothered him before, but now the threat seemed real. The world, to Harry O'Keeffe, had become a threatening place, and who knew what else it might have in store for his family?

'Maybe it is to do with the baby. This has been happening more since the baby arrived too.'

At bedtime, Bernadette lit the red candle under the Sacred Heart picture hanging over the kitchen table.

'I will leave this lighting all night; maybe it will help. We will all kneel and say the rosary at ten o'clock.'

And they did. The rosary started with Bernadette beginning the first decade, the rest of the family following on with the reply. And then they went to bed.

And perhaps it worked. There was not a sound in the house that night, as all of them slept more soundly than they had for some weeks. Even baby Gertrude.

★ ★ ★

In Bruff, the first Friday in every of the month was fair day.

Animals were brought to the centre of town, where everyone gathered who had anything to sell. The town was packed with pigs, cattle, hens and rabbits, the latter hung over a wire line. The smell of them was, to Richie, unbelievable. Sheep were shepherded into corners with wooden planks. Local farmers walked viewed the animals with a critical eye before haggling to get a good bargain from the sellers. Deals were struck, generally confirmed with a spit on the hand before offering it to the other party.

Bruff had come to life, and was teeming with people. The teahouse was full to the door, while the public house was brimming with thirsty men. Local townspeople made a killing when the fair day came around. Anything from a needle to an anchor could be sold, and generally was.

This also presented an opportunity to the women, of course. Unmarried women came out in droves, and cast critical eyes of their own over lines of prospective husbands. They generally stood together in groups, laughing and sniggering, a bit shy to approach any man. Not armed with planks of wood, they would throw a glad eye in the direction of a man who looked single and free. Such men were generally in the company of their fathers, helping them with the buying and selling whilst soaking up the atmosphere, and perhaps daring to hope that an eye or two would be cast in their direction.

When night fell, the rubbish from the day would remain on the street, only to be cleared away by the rain.

Richie enjoyed walking along the stalls and chatting to everyone. The people there were all doing some sort of business, much of which was entirely new to him. The locals loved hearing his American accent, and he was something of a celebrity in the town. While walking along, seeing and being seen, he came across Tom, the hackney man, who was in town for the fair. Richie was delighted to meet Tom; it was like meeting an old friend again.

Tom, it turned out, knew more than Richie did about what was happening in Bruff. He knew that the O'Keeffes were in deep trouble with the payments to the landlord. And he knew that five or more families in Bruff were in a similar predicament.

'You are very well informed. How and where do you hear all this?

'Sure, news goes around here, especially when a farmer is in trouble with payments. It's important to know these things.'

'What will happen to the O'Keeffe family?'

'They won't have long before they are turned out of their home unless they can make payments and clear their arrears. The men and women that live on the land are proud people, and they love what they do.'

This news hit Richie hard.

'But what do you know about the O'Keeffes? Are they going to manage?'

'All I know is that they are on the list of evictions. The way it usually goes is that the sons get out and emigrate. It lessens the burden on the family. They can usually send some money back. Most children who have gone away do.'

'It's a shame to see families broken up like this.'

'Oh yes. But sure what choice do you have? They should have done it years ago if you ask me. I don't know what's wrong with Harry, maybe he can't part with them.'

'Who could blame him?'

'Delaying the inevitable will only make things more difficult, Mr Fitzgerald. Maybe you should chat with them about this, make them see sense.'

'I will do what I can,' Richie said. 'But I don't know if it is my place to tell somebody how to live like that. I wouldn't thank somebody for telling me what I must do. They are my friends.'

'True enough, sure,' Tom said. 'But a friend is somebody who can tell you the truth even when you don't want to hear it. Friends who can't do that are more trouble than they're worth.'

'I will drive out there tomorrow and see what I can do.'

'Will you come and have a glass with me in the porterhouse? It'll be full today, so; sure there'll be some fun to be had.'

About that, he was right. A heavy smell of sweat and urine permeated the place, as did the carnival atmosphere. Both men had a few pints of porter.

'That's probably enough for me, Tom. I'm not much of a drinker, really.'

'Sure, neither am I,' said Tom.

The pub's owner was not keen for them to depart.

'Lads, it's only getting started. We will have music and dancing in a short while. You wouldn't want to miss it now.'

He set down two pints of porter in front of the men in with an air of finality and in the knowledge of a point well made.

'Sure, you wouldn't want to miss all the fun,' opined another man. 'The women are waiting outside for us.'

'I have my wife and family at home in Limerick,' said Tom in a half-hearted protest.

'I have a wife and family too, sure. But a man who has a drink can still see what's on offer, can he not?'

Richie and Tom found that they were powerless to resist the logic of this. Even so, their drinks finished, they made their way out of the porterhouse. The man inside had not been lying: several ladies had assembled outside, and were ready and waiting for defenceless men to depart the establishment. These ladies were not shy, and giggled and smiled at all passing men. They were old pros at this game, afraid of nothing. They put their arms around Richie and Tom as another of their group started an Irish jig on an instrument that looked to Richie like a kind of banjo as the others clapped along enthusiastically. It was all that Tom and Richie could do to make their escape, but escape they did.

'Jesus, but it would be easy to get involved with this lot of women, what so you think, Richie?'

'Not me, thanks.'

It took some time for the men to get back to O'Sullivan's. People everywhere were asking them to buy some of their goods. 'Have a look around, sir: we have fine wool for knitting pullovers!' 'Polish for your boots, sir?' Another stall wanted him to buy boots and socks. They had tailors measuring up for three-piece suits, which they would have ready for next month's fair for collection. The men were laughing and joking at the spectacle of it all.

Back in his room that night, Richie pondered on his conversation with Tom about the O'Keeffes' situation. There

was really no way out of this debt for them. He could pay
off the amount owed, of course, but then there would be
next month's rent due. How would they pay that? The only
thing for it was for their sons to get tickets for their passage
to America. He could organise work, and a place for them
to stay in Boston. That would at least give them a start. He
had a friend in the building trade, and the boys would be
able to pick that up quickly enough.

Richie fell asleep on top of the bed, and woke during
the night, freezing with the cold. He had been dreaming
that the O'Keeffe family had been evicted and were setting out to America. Harry, Bernadette, Aoife and baby
Gertrude.

He had it in his head that he would suggest this the
next day to the family, but did not hold out much hope
of Harry agreeing to leave Ireland to begin a new life in
another country so far away. Harry had his heart and soul
in Ireland.

When Richie arrived at the O'Keeffes', dinner was
already underway, with Harry in his usual position at the
head of the table.

'Pull up a chair; I put on an extra bit of dinner thinking
you might call,' Bernadette said.

He joined the family at their table, and made small talk
about the weather and how things were going with the
livestock. Nothing too serious. As dinner drew to an end,
Richie saw his chance to raise the subject.

'I had a dream last night. It is a significant dream, and I
think maybe a way out for you and the family.'

He looked in Harry's direction. Harry lit his pipe and
looked back at Richie, his eyes focussed.

'Can you work miracles too?' Harry asked.

'I would if I could,' he said, smiling. 'But I do have a
suggestion for all of you.'

Everyone stopped what they were doing. Richie had their attention.

'Well now this is only a suggestion, and it requires a lot of thought. It's for the whole family together. I am thinking that you should consider—all of you—leaving Ireland for a new start abroad. Like in Boston.'

There was silence. Not a word was spoken by anybody. Harry puffed on his pipe, contemplatively.

'Yes,' said Bernadette, breaking the uncomfortable silence. 'We should consider everything. Harry and I are not young, but we are fit and healthy, and not afraid of work. Do you think I would get work over there?'

'Yes,' Richie said. 'There are many jobs in housekeeping, and you are certainly an expert in that!'

Harry said nothing. The sons were beaming from ear to ear.

'The boys might be able to find work building houses. I have a friend who owns a building firm, and he is looking for good, strong young men. The pay is good, but the hours are long.'

Harry's sons did not entirely take after their father.

'It would be wonderful to work over there,' they said, almost in unison.

'... love to emigrate ...'

'... earn some decent money ...'

'... at least there is some work over there ...'

'Sure, it isn't like we don't work hard here!'

But then Aoife spoke up.

'And what about Gertrude? Would she like Boston? What would her life be over there?'

'She is very small; she won't mind where she is so long as she is with you, Aoife,' said Bernadette.

Harry remained silent. Richie knew that Harry would prefer to think and ponder on the matter for a long time, but time was not on their side. It could not be easy to think of leaving his farm and lands. But he really didn't own anything any more. He was in a difficult situation, and this offered the best hope of a way out.

'You wouldn't be on your own,' said Richie. 'I would be with you every step of the way. It is a lot of steps, but I would be with you for all them.'

Harry turned white in the face, stood, and left the kitchen. He returned to the table after a short while. He looked around the table while his family waited for him to say something.

'I never wanted to leave Ireland. When I was a young man, many of my friends and neighbours left for foreign shores. I wanted to make a go of it here in Bruff, and felt very proud of myself when I got this farm. Bernadette was introduced to me by the matchmaker Billy Butler, Lord rest his soul. We hit it off from the start, and we still hit it off well. I could not bear to see her and our children without a home or a roof over our heads. I am ashamed of the fact that we cannot pay the rent to the landlord. I see no way of doing so either. It won't be long until the sheriff will come and put a notice on our door too: 'Tenants Out'.

He looked sorrowfully at Richie.

'There is nothing else for it; we will have to leave for America. I think that it's the best thing for all of us. They will have a decent living there. I know I would prefer not to leave, but our circumstances dictate that we go. There are many farmers here who will be evicted, and they won't have this chance. Richie … you are some sort of blessing from God for helping us like this, truly you are. That's all I have to say.'

Everyone was shocked to hear this from Harry, including Richie.

Bernadette spoke. 'Are you sure, Harry?'

'I am. What else can we do? Sure we have nothing to lose. We will rise to the challenge and make a go of it in Boston. It will be good for the boys, and Aoife too.'

'I will start making arrangements, then,' said Richie.

'Do that,' Harry agreed.

'It could take a month or so before everything is arranged.'

Harry nodded.

'Thank you. Thank you for everything.'

As Richie left the O'Keeffes' home later that night, Harry walked down to the road gate with him.

'Keep all this to yourself,' he said. 'I don't know that I want everybody to know our business.'

'Well, the shipping company will need your names, ages and addresses and such. There isn't much we can do about that. I have been here for long enough to know that everybody knows everybody; there aren't a lot of secrets around here. But I'll do my best. I won't answer any questions from nosey neighbours.'

'Good man,' He tapped Richie on the shoulder.

20.

A dense fog engulfed Bruff and the surrounding environs during the night. You couldn't see your hand in front of you. It remained for the following day, and never lifted that night either. Everything came to a standstill. On the third morning at about eleven o'clock, the sun broke through, lifting the fog for a few hours.

Richie took the chance to go to the shipping office and enquire about the next ship to the United States. He was advised that there were no ships leaving port while the fog lasts.

'What about in a month's time? We will be into late April then.'

'Yes, sir,' replied the clerk. 'We have a ship travelling from Queenstown to Liverpool. It will be one day's wait for the ship to Boston from there.'

'Are you booked up for that ship?'

'No, sir. We have plenty of room. Are you looking for the bottom of the ship or standing on deck?'

'I am looking for three cabins; a family of six, and a single one as well.'

The clerk had heard such things before.

'I will send off a request for you. Come back in a week and I will have some details for you.'

★ ★ ★

The O'Keeffes were sitting around the fire, discussing their future. They had a roaring fire on as it was cold and damp outside. Harry was smoking his pipe while Bernadette was asking a lot of questions about how it would be in another country — questions that none of them was well equipped to answer.

'Whatever happens, we will all be together,' she said. 'That is the most important thing. So long as we are all together, we'll be all right.'

Aoife talked about little Gertrude and how it would be for her. She would get to go to a good school and have nice clothes to wear. The boys were more interested in the prospect of having work, money and a good time.

The baby started to cry an unmerciful screeching cry. Aoife picked her up in her arms, but the baby was stretched out so stiffly that Aoife struggled to hold her properly. Bernadette stretched out her arms to take the baby from Aoife and try to content her. The baby seemed to be in awful pain.

'Maybe it's only wind.' Bernadette put Gertrude up on her shoulder and patted her on the back. The kitchen door blew open and banged against the wall. Wind came down the chimney and put fire, smoke and ashes all over the floor and on everyone sitting there. The second burst of wind went straight up to the roof of the house beside the chimney and left a gaping hole in the roof of the house.

Bernadette hurried to clean the baby while Harry closed the kitchen door. The boys and Aoife stood there, stunned. When the wind died down, Aoife spoke.

'Now I know Harry said it's the spirit of this house who is angry and probably does not like us leaving and taking the baby away. I have heard that there was a spirit of a young woman here in this house years ago. She died tragically when she was about to deliver her second baby.

Maybe that's the woman who sits at the end of my bed every night. She watches over Gertrude. She is happy with this woman and smiles at her.'

In unison, Harry and Bernadette asked, 'What woman?'

'You know, Mammy, the one who comes at night. Haven't you seen her at the end of the bed ? She told me she is Gertrude's guardian angel. I am happy she is an angel because my little baby will be safe with her and with us at night.'

'Well she is very angry now,' Harry said. 'I didn't know anything about this angel. Where does she come from?'

'I have no idea, Dad. She is just there always.'

'Even when you had no baby?'

'Yes, she has been with me all the time, as far back as I can remember. I didn't want anyone to know about her, although since Mammy came to sleep with us I thought she had seen her too.'

'Well now … Jesus …' Harry said. 'There is a woman in this house that I know nothing about?'

'Well I didn't know either,' said Bernadette.

'Ah, it's just your imagination,' said Harry, looking at Aoife.

She shouted back to her father, 'She is very real to me! She is my friend all the time. I don't want her to leave this house. If we have to go, I want her to come with me.'

It occurred to Harry that his daughter's invisible friend would probably not require a ticket, but he thought it better to say nothing.

'She wouldn't want to leave here anyway. She is only in your mind,' said Bernadette.

Aoife clammed up and didn't say another word. She got the feeling this woman she knew well wasn't real, or a real person.

The next day, Harry and the boys got some straw, reeds and sedge from the swamp so as to thatch over the gaping hole. The thatching was a skilled job, and usually done by Jim Walsh, who thatched everyone's home in the surrounding area. But there was no time to get Jim. Harry and the boys made a good job of filling the hole in the roof, just in time to keep the torrential rains out. The boys cut the bundles of straw and reeds to the required length and selected the stronger ones. They passed the bundles to their father, who secured the thatch. The job was done. Harry didn't know if it would hold if the strange weather they had been experiencing should return.

Harry spoke to Bernadette that night as they sat by the fireside before they went to bed. Bernadette was uneasy that there could be a spirit in the house. Either Aoife had lost her mind, or there was some strange presence, sitting at the end or her daughter's bed every night. Neither prospect was at all appealing.

'Well,' Harry said, as gently as he could, 'there is nothing you can do or I can do either. If there is a spirit in this house, it was here before we came here. It could take a hundred years for this unhappy soul to cross over to the next world.'

'Maybe closure of whatever happened here is what is needed,' said Bernadette, thoughtfully. 'It's our young daughter Aoife who it has attached to. When we leave this house everything should work out for the best. We will have to live with it until then. I don't want any more holes in the roof.'

'Me neither,' Harry agreed enthusiastically, looking at his bruised hands. 'That wind is so strong it could move a mountain.'

★ ★ ★

While Richie Fitzgerald looked after their passage to Boston, the family got things together. Many things had to be left behind, like furniture and bedding. Richie advised them that they would have everything they needed when they arrived in Boston. 'Just bring what is dear to you, like family photographs and things that were handed down; things that you care about.' That had been his advice, over the course of their many long talks about the subject.

The community of Bruff and beyond got word that the O'Keeffes were leaving Ireland for America. Not many of them lacked an opinion on the matter, or cared to keep it to themselves. No one could believe that Harry O'Keeffe would leave and emigrate—he was the one man they thought would never leave Bruff. Even so, many understood his situation and were in a similar one themselves. It was no small matter to be behind on the rent and unable to come up with the money. Some farming families thought it was very brave of Harry to go out into the unknown and make a new start abroad with his family. Some of the wives were jealous of Bernadette, who was leaving them behind for a new life. Others were critical of her, feeling that she should encourage her family to stay and manage somehow.

As for Bernadette's own feelings, she cherished the chance to leave and begin a new life with her family.

Bernadette talked at length to Aoife about the new life in America. Aoife had even less sense than she did of what it would be like to live there. Bernadette had been in contact via letters from her friends who had made the journey years before. She clung to the thought that they would all be together, and that together they would somehow manage.

Aoife's feelings were mixed. It seemed unfair on baby Gertrude that she would have to endure the long voyage. After they arrived, what kind of life would Boston be able to offer her? Aoife knew that it was likely to be better than what was on offer there in Bruff, but the prospect of being surrounded with unfamiliar things was daunting for a girl who had never been more than a few miles from where she had been born.

The boys, of course, could not wait for the day when they would leave. They were so excited and ready for the day to come, the sooner, the better.

It was perhaps hardest for Harry, who spent long evenings chatting to the men of the community about how and why he decided to leave. Some other men were thinking of leaving also. When Harry O'Keeffe could set off and leave, maybe they could too. But none of these men had the money for the fare, let alone somewhere to live after they actually arrived. It was, for them, no more than a dream—and of course a thing to talk about idly over a few pints of porter whilst passing the time as agreeably as it could be passed at that place and in that time.

Two men decided to leave on the same day, on the same boat, as the O'Keeffes. They were not taking their wives and families until they had a job and were earning enough money to find a house, as well as the fare over for those they had left behind. It was the best they could do. They planned to send money home every week to their families. They knew, though, that there could be times when the money stopped coming in—with no husband and no money, their wives would curse their names.

Richie got word from the shipping company that there was a ship leaving for Liverpool on April 20th. The O'Keeffes had four weeks to get everything together. Harry went to the fair day in Bruff, taking his pigs, goats and cattle for sale. He sold everything and made a handsome sum. He even took the boys into the pub and bought them a glass of porter each. It was served in a tall and narrow glass. The porter was as black as ink with a creamy white top. 'Drink it up,' Harry said, 'it will put hairs on your chest.' They did their best because if they chickened out they would be children in Harry's mind. The boys couldn't understand why every man liked this black stuff. They asked their father, who replied, 'It's a required taste.' He did not mean 'acquired'.

Men of the town came over to Harry to wish him well in America. They were all in awe of Harry O'Keeffe—the man they thought they knew well. A man who worked hard and loved the land. A man to whom they went for advice on everything and anything. They told him he would be sadly missed in the community. Who would they go to now for advice? 'Go to the solicitor in Bruff,' he advised them. But he knew they could not afford his services. 'There is always someone who can give you advice. Sure, mine's probably not worth having anyway.' Harry recommended Billy Byrne — 'That man is a mine of information, although he does not let anyone know what he knows, but when I am gone I'm sure he will step into my shoes and help everyone. He won't give wrong advice; I know that for sure.'

As he stepped out of the pub, there was a crowd around Harry, the news of him leaving had spread near and far. Some men were sympathising with him on being behind with the rent; they knew the landlord was about to send in the sheriff to close the farm down and evict the family. Others were congratulating him on his courage to leave everything behind and start again in America. His reply to them was, 'It's never too late to begin again.'

Men enquired after how his wife and family felt about the move. 'They are all delighted,' he told them.

'Jaysus, but she is a great woman! You are lucky to have her!'

Most knew about his daughter, Aoife, but they did not mention her to Harry. They knew that his daughter was a tragedy and did not want to remind him of this. Of course there were some people in the neighbourhood who had bad things to say about the O'Keeffes, how Harry was the big fella who knew everything and was unable to look after his own affairs. But they were few and far between.

Richie Fitzgerald thought he would have a hard job convincing him to move to the United States, but it had not proved to be too difficult. He was so very pleased for the family. He reminded Harry that he was doing the best thing for his wife and family.

Sitting at the fire almost every night, Bernadette would chat with Harry. The topic had changed from Aoife to their new life in America. She confided in Harry that when she was a young woman she dreamt of emigrating to the US or Canada. Some of her school friends went to Australia. Whole families left and went to foreign shores to make a living. She knew that when they left they had never seen their friends and the rest of her families again, and that was what had prevented her from trying to leave as well. She could not bear the thought of leaving her parents and her sisters and brothers. She told Harry that she was glad she did not go because she would never have met him if she did.

'Well, Bernadette,' he said, 'I secretly wanted to go and follow my friends also. Being the only one left at home wasn't easy. My mother and father would not hear tell of me going. I was happy in the end, and stayed to help out my parents. If Richie hadn't arrived here, we wouldn't be able to go now. It's great for our family ... we don't have to part with any of them. We can all be together, and that is all that matters.'

Bernadette was near to tears listening to Harry and his love for his family.

All of Bruff knew that Richie was soon to leave and take the O'Keeffes with him to the States. Each time he stepped out of O'Sullivan's, young men and women stopped to chat with him and ask about a possible passage to the US. The young that were left in Bruff had ambitions to emigrate and make a new life away from Ireland as there was no way that they could see of making a decent living where they were.

Richie would advise them to save the fare, promising to stay in touch and that he would do what he could to help them when they got to America. People and friends of his and his family would set up an organisation to help with finding work and get them settled in apartments and flats.

Some of the young people of Bruff were very fortunate indeed to have Richie Fitzgerald to help them.

★ ★ ★

Brendan O'Keeffe's conscience was troubled. How was he going to tell the Brotherhood that he was going to emigrate to America? How was he going to tell Seanie? Having finally found a cause that he believed in, was he really going to abandon it? There was nothing for it though: Seanie had to be told of his plans.

When Brendan arrived to see Seanie, he found him guarding the canvas bag, as he expected. When he told him about his family's plans, Seanie was distraught.

'You can't just leave the B… B… Brotherhood behind, Bren. We are your family too.'

'I'm not leaving it all behind. I'll be able to help from America. I can send things that you can't get here. You'll see.'

'You're abandoning us.'

'Seanie … your stammer. It has almost gone.'

'It hasn't g… gone. It's because I'm angry.'

'Besides, I don't know how much help we can be, Seanie. They think we're both eejits, not just you. Did you ever look inside the bag?'

'They told me not to.'

'Have a look, so.'

'No, we *can't*.'

'We can.'

Brendan brushed the straw off the bag. Seanie pushed him away hard as he grabbed it, and the bag flew open, spilling its contents noisily onto the ground between them. It was saucepans and bedding.

'You see, Seanie, they don't trust us with guns.'

'Bren, they …'

'Fuck it anyway. My bag was much the same.'

'This stuff could be important, B… B… Bren. They could need supplies at any time. They do trust us, they just can't …'

'What?'

'They can't give a… a… anybody who comes along g… g… guns, can they?'

'Maybe you're right. This stuff could save their lives. Catch a rabbit or a pheasant or something.' Brendan poked around at the ground dejectedly. 'There's nothing else to be done, sure.'

'Not n… nothing, Bren. There's a dance at Byrne's tonight. L… Let's go.'

'Why not?'

21.

The Quirkes and the Stauntons attended Mass every Sunday morning, just like everyone else in the community. Although they sat far away from one another, they could end up beside one another going up to Holy Communion. Many a sermon from the priest recommended forgiveness of one's neighbours, but this advice was generally not taken to heart.

In such a community, what might look to an outsider like a small grievance could assume a large significance, at least in the minds of the people involved.

When the oldest of the Quirkes, Tom, took ill and died, Mrs Staunton went up to the door and gave her condolences to Jim. He dismissed her and told her to go away. Both families were growing old and getting feeble in their way. They thought they would last forever and work like they used to do.

A bad flu-like sickness took many elderly people in Bruff and around the whole country. Not many old people survived the sickness. Four more living in the same lane were buried that springtime. They were all over seventy years old. This left others to keep the feud going, which they were fairly willing to do. The heart never went out of the devilment.

Things were changing on the lane very gradually, if at all. Grass grew along the centre of the lane. There was little traffic to keep it from doing so.

★ ★ ★

Richie was busy making arrangements for the O'Keeffes. All of his time was taken up with the details. One night he decided to retire early to his room, intending finally to read the remaining letters kept in the bottom drawer of his cupboard. The night was getting dark, and it looked like it was about to rain. He lit the lamp in his bedroom and turned up the wick so it would give more light. Sitting on the side of his bed, he sifted through the letters. Selecting one that looked like it was of a personal nature, he opened the envelope. The paper inside was very light.

Dick Fitzgerald, you have been on my mind all my life, we went to school together up until the age of ten. You never looked at me, nor did anyone else in the school. I was tall for my age, and I know boys and girls didn't like the look of me. But I knew I was the best-looking girl in Bruff, although I did not do well at reading and writing. I made the tea for everyone during the winter and kept the fire in the school room going all the time—that was my job. I remember the Master telling me that the fire was the most important job in all the school.

I walked to school and home from school by myself, although I didn't get to school every day— my mother died when I was only a baby, and my brothers looked after me as best they could until I was able to take care of myself. They told me to keep well away from men. I didn't understand, because I liked men and they liked me too! I was happiest when I had men around me.

It was you, Dick Fitzgerald, who I wanted. I tried everything to get you. I often called to your house on a sunny Sunday afternoon. All you could tell me was to go home out of that. There was one Sunday I came across you in the barn, and that day you were friendly to me. We made love in that barn, and you were the happiest man in the world, you said. I never told anyone what happened between us because I wanted it to happen again. When it didn't, it saddened me.

I want you to know that I had a baby child by you, and left him outside the church in Limerick. I couldn't take home a baby to the house—my brothers would kill me. I had more babies, and did the same thing. I hope that they all had a good life. I named him Dick, after you. Do you know anyone called Dick who would be about thirty years old by now? I suppose you wouldn't look at him anyway. Maybe he looks like you.

Anyway, I am getting beat up now and not out much around the fields, so I don't have any men calling like they used to do. I have a lot of time to think about what happened. If you had married me I would have been so happy, and would not have the want for men like I used to do. Isn't that a pity now—the two of us could have lived happy ever after. My name would be Mrs Fitzgerald, and very proud to be your wife. You are the only man I am writing to because you still haunt my mind.

I was so sorry for you and the children when your first wife, Catherine, died. You looked so sad. Your next wife, young Margaret Dillon, wasn't suitable for you at all. I knew what happened to her, and her goings on with the workman, Mr James. I often heard the two of them in the middle of the night out in the barn. James was savage for her. He only had me when Margaret wasn't around. I wanted to tell you what I felt for you, but couldn't because you were with everyone else and nobody wanted me near them. My heart was broken for you, Dick. Then, when I called to your house, you didn't want to see me. That was pitiful.

People have told me that you are not well and don't go out any more—that's why I am writing to you. Well, I am getting someone to do this for me as you know I am not good at it at all myself. My old bones are sore and tired, and I prefer to sit by the fire and cook a bit of dinner for my brothers.

Goodbye, Dick Fitzgerald. Maybe I will see you in the next world.

Your friend,

Mary.

Richie laid his head back on the bed, trying to take it all in. He felt he was intruding on his ancestor's life. He felt sorry for this woman, and for Dick too. He was concerned to hear of a possible relation left outside a hospital in Limerick. But then, perhaps the baby was not Dick Fitzgerald's at all. He was not going to ask anyone about this woman—probably she had gone to the next world and was not around any more. This letter may have been the last letter she got her friend to write for her.

He decided to tear it up and burn it with the lighted candle. There was no need for anyone else to read this letter. He made a decision there and then not to open the remaining two letters. He put them back in the drawer of the dressing table.

★ ★ ★

The O'Keeffes couldn't wait for the day to come to leave Ireland and make a new life for themselves. Everyone was shocked at Harry O'Keeffe, who was a man who loved the land, loved Ireland, and most of all loved Bruff. None of his neighbours and friends could understand his excitement at leaving for America. Some thought him too old and advanced in years to make a new start over there. Others were delighted for him and how he was handling the eviction from his home and farm.

The Byrnes, his friends and neighbours were putting on an American wake party for Harry and his family. People came from miles around to celebrate and mourn them. They knew they would never see them again. At least, not in this life they would not.

All the O'Keeffes attended the party/wake, except Aoife, who was not allowed to go. Harry gave instructions that she was to stay at home with her baby. She pleaded with her father to let her go with Gertrude. The baby, she said, would sleep all the time anyway. But it was a definite no from Harry. Aoife asked for an explanation from her father as to why or what was the reason she could not attend. Harry would not explain any further. Bernadette offered that she would stay at home with Aoife and the baby. Harry would not hear tell of it. Bernadette was to join him at the Byrne's. 'You are my wife. When I ask you to go to places with me, you will come, and there is no more to be said about it.'

Harry had gone into the town of Bruff and ordered some wooden chests for their belongings, even though most of the things they were bringing were for the baby, plus a few ornaments and keepsakes Bernadette had. Her mother had given her a wedding present of a tea and full dinner set in bone china, which she never used. There was also some silver cutlery her Aunt Hazel had given her for a wedding present. Richie picked up the chests and delivered them to the O'Keeffe's.

As the day went by, Bernadette and Aoife got everything together and stacked them in the right order in the chest.

The party night at the Byrne's came around quickly. Harry and Bernadette put on their best clothes, as did their sons. These same clothes would be the ones they would dress in for the long voyage. The Byrnes had the biggest crowd in the house that they ever had. As the O'Keeffes walked up the lane, it was lined with donkeys and carts and some horses and traps.

'I never saw so many carts and traps before at Byrne's!' said Harry.

When they got to the door of the house, people were spilling out onto the yard. Men and women started clapping as they entered the house. The music and dancing, which had already begun, stopped when they entered the room. Everyone turned to cheer and clap for the O'Keeffes. Bernadette, who was a bit shy, went a bit red-faced. Harry, on the other hand, lapped it up. A pint glass of porter quickly landed in his hand, while a glass of lemonade was given to Bernadette. Bridget sat on the wooden bench beside the wall that they referred to as 'the furm', which she shared with three other ladies from the region. They had many questions for Bernadette. Some she could not answer, but others she was happy to.

When Richie Fitzgerald entered the room, Bernadette could see all the women gazing at him—the single ones,

and most of the married ones too. They were all in agreement that he was a very handsome man, and that the
woman who got him would be well looked after.

Moira Dunphy said to Bernadette, 'He is all mine.
Watch this.' She walked straight over to him and asked
him for the next dance. Richie, defenceless, agreed to this.
They stepped out together onto the dancing area that was
responsible for almost half of Bruff's population.

'I am not the best to dance,' said Richie.

'That's no problem at all,' Moira reassured him. 'Follow
my steps and you will be fine.'

Richie did just that. At the end of the dance, Moira
hung on to Richie and suggested they would dance again
as she thought the next dance would be a foxtrot, which
was slower.

'Hold me like this,' she advised, pulling Richie within
the range of her feminine charms.

'I might have a break and sit this one out, actually,' said
Richie. 'You could ask one of those men standing over
there.'

She glanced in the direction he had indicated.

'That lot are useless! All they want is to make babies.
That's all they think about. Not gentlemen like you.'

Richie couldn't hold back a loud laugh, which annoyed
Moira.

'Ah, you are just the same as them. I thought you had
it in you to love a nice woman like me.'

'I love all women, of course I do, but I have not met
anyone special yet, or should I say no one special has come
to me yet. Anyhow, I have plenty of time. I am a young
man; where's the rush?'

Moira walked away and returned to her circle of
friends, who were excited to find out what the conversation was between her and Richie. Moira relayed it all to

the women, who agreed that he was more trouble than he was worth.

The night moved along, and the party saw the sun rise. Everybody was in high spirits. But when the party came to its end, it was time to say their goodbyes to Harry and Bernadette. This proved to be too much for some of the friends who had known them for a lifetime. Women were crying and hugging and kissing Bernadette. Men offered a firm handshake by way of their final farewell. It was emotional for Richie to witness a family leaving for good.

Returning home to the O'Keeffes' home, things were quiet and a darkness came over the house. Harry studied the chests on the kitchen floor, some filled and some half-filled. He couldn't quite believe what they were all about to do. Were they forgetting to bring anything with them that they would need? Not that he could think of. Truth to tell, they did not have a great deal of possessions. His pipe collection would come with him, of course, as would his favourite tobacco pouch. But his wheelbarrow, despite being very useful, would probably not be needed in the New World. His spade and brush would need to be left for the farm's next owner in the barn. He went to pay them a visit, labouring under porter-fuelled emotions. Brandy the dog followed him as usual. At which point it occurred to Harry, for the first time, that his faithful friend would not be able to accompany them to Boston. He made an about-turn of which a military man would be proud, and headed to the kitchen, where all of the family's quarrels and disputes were resolved.

On returning to the kitchen, he looked at Bernadette, and could see the lost look in her eyes. He knew that she did not truly want to leave, and would rather have stayed where her friends were. This was the only life she had ever known. She would not say such a thing to Harry, of course, and he knew it. They had little choice about the matter.

All that day, Harry did not have any work to do on the farm. He had too much time to think about leaving. He spent most of the day sitting in the barn. It was empty; the animals had been sold. It felt so lonely. The silence was broken when Bernadette called him in for his dinner.

Harry sat in his chair at the head of the table, staring down at his dinner with the knife and fork in his hands.

'Is your dinner okay?' Bernadette asked.

'Yes, it's fine. I have no hunger on me today is all. When a man is out working hard, he is eager to have his dinner no matter what is put up in front of him.'

He pushed his chair back from the table and stood. He wanted to breathe some fresh air.

'I will leave it beside the fire. Maybe you will be hungry later on tonight,' said Bernadette.

'I doubt it,' he said, making his way outside.

Later that night, Bernadette found him sitting on some straw on the barn floor. She sat beside him.

'What is it, Harry?'

'I am thinking about leaving everything I ever had behind me. I am feeling lost. There is nothing here in the barn to take care of, no milking, no goats to get Brandy to bring home. This place is so empty without the animals, and there is nothing for me to do. We've put in so much is all, Bern. So much....'

'Come on now, Harry. We are moving on and up in the world. We are all going to a better place, and we will have a good living over there. You can go out and do a day's work and get paid for it, and so can the boys. We won't have to struggle like this any more. We will manage.'

'You're right.' He nodded appreciatively.

'We will do more than manage: we will be great over there, you'll see. We need to have courage now, for all of us.'

'I know you are right. It just isn't easy.'

'I will cook and keep house, and maybe do a few hours every day housekeeping for some rich people, so all in all we will be better off than trying to stay here.'

'I don't know what it is about leaving its breaking my heart. It's getting in on me. At Byrne's the other night everyone was so happy for us getting the chance to make a new life, but all I wanted was my life here, where I was born. I couldn't let anyone know what I was thinking. Am I a failure, Bernadette?'

'Of course you fecking aren't! You married me.' She put her arm around his shoulders. 'I don't know about you, but I am looking forward to leaving and starting over again in a new land.'

'Ah, it's different for you women.'

'Less proud than you are, you mean?'

'You tell me.'

'Well now, Harry, I have never complained, have I? I worked and did my best with what I had. And sometimes that was not much at all. We all thought you were happy to leave. You said so yourself. That's the impression I got, anyway.'

'I got caught up in the excitement and the offer from Richie Fitzgerald of taking us to his homeland. I don't know what I am going to do now.'

'You are coming with us, and that's that,' Bernadette said. 'There is no going back on your promise now, Harry. There is nothing here for us any more. Soon the sheriff will be here with his gang of men. They will take everything and put you out on the road to live. This is just last-minute nerves is all. We need to be strong for them.' She gestured in the direction of the farmhouse.

Hand in hand, they went back into the house, where Harry sat beside the fire with his head in his hands. He sat like this for hours. Bernadette had baked two big cakes of brown soda bread and had to move around him to get to the fire.

'Come on now, Harry,' Bernadette suggested. 'It's time to go to bed for the night. Maybe you will feel better tomorrow. Hope and peace for your new beginnings.'

Harry still sat there. Bernadette shook him.

'I will be up behind you,' he said. 'You go ahead.'

'Don't stay long down here. The fire is going out and you will get cold.'

'I will be on soon,' he said, with a tone that permitted no further complaint or discussion of the matter.

Bernadette woke during the night. Harry was not beside her. She went down to the kitchen, only to find him asleep head-down on the kitchen table. He had some writing paper, a pen and ink, and had clearly intended to write something. But what?

'Come on, you,' Bernadette said, squeezing his arm gently.

'Wha? I'm fine.'

'You are not, Harry. Now tell me, what are you writing here? Don't worry me like this.'

'I was writing to my relatives to let them know we are leaving for America. Only I must have fallen asleep....'

'Yes, you must've. Come on, let's get you to bed.'

'Sure there's no harm done; I will come with you now.'

'Everybody who knows us knows where we are going. Sure they were all at the Byrne's!'

Harry did not sleep well that night, and tossed and turned until morning. When he awoke the next morning, he set off to milk the cows, before remembering that they no longer had any.

'Oh God, I'm so used to getting up and doing the milking I forgot myself.'

'You really don't know what you're doing, do you?' said Bernadette.

'I certainly don't know what I will spend the day doing.'

'Well I do,' said Bernadette. 'You get the chest, and finish packing. Take only what you think you will use over there, don't bring a whole load of things you won't ever use again.'

It was obvious to Bernadette that something was concerning Harry. Something in addition to his last-minute nerves. But she did not know what it could possibly be.

'More second thoughts? she asked him.

'Its hard to go and leave everything you have at my age,' he replied.

'*Our* age. Come on now,' said Bernadette, 'aren't you the lucky man to have your wife and family who are willing to go and make a new life for ourselves. And especially Richie Fitzgerald, who is more than willing to help us.'

'I'll be all right when it comes to it. We will go, and have no regrets about anything.'

On the following night, Harry sat up late again. And once again, Bernadette came down to see that he was all right. He had the pen and ink out on the table again with some white notepaper. When he heard her footsteps he hurried to hide what he was writing.

'Still writing letters? Sure you must have written to everyone in Ireland by now.'

'You go on back to bed; I will follow you when I am finished here. This is the only quiet time I really get. Everybody is too busy and there is too much noise most of the time. I just need a bit of time to myself for this. I don't want to forget anyone or leave anyone out is all.'

Bernadette went back to bed.

In the morning, when she woke, Harry was not beside her. He must have fallen asleep at the table again, she thought. He will be tired all day long now. When she was dressed and went down to the kitchen, Harry was not there either. The pen and paper were back in the cupboard where they were kept. She started the fire and put the kettle on for the cup of tea. She made a pot of porridge, and waited for him to return from wherever he was.

Aoife was up for breakfast before Bernadette had finished making it, and the boys too. When Bernadette began to serve breakfast, there was still no sign of Harry. The boys suggested that he must have gone for a walk with Brandy. But Brandy was soon found lying in the sunshine outside the front door, as was his habit. 'He is waiting for father to return,' Aoife said.

'When we are finished here I will have a look and see where he is,' Bernadette said. She tried to sound as if she wasn't worried, but she felt a bit concerned. It was not like Harry to disappear off like this. She put her coat on and called the dog to follow her.

As she approached the barn, the dog began to bark and fidget. There was something hanging from the tree beside the barn. Bernadette knew what it was before she had properly seen it, and ran to him, trying to prop up his feet and remove the rope from his neck. His tongue was protruding from his mouth, and it was as black as coal. His eyes were bulging from their sockets. She tried to hold onto him, keeping him up in her arms. But it was hopeless. His body was already stiff. Brandy circled around him frantically, somehow understanding the significance of what had happened.

Bernadette heard Richie Fitzgerald's car coming up the lane, and ran out to him.

'Richie! Harry is dead! He has … he has hanged himself. What am I going to do now?'

Richie went into the barn and got the handsaw to cut the rope. When he did so, Harry fell to the ground with a lifeless thud. Brandy the dog came over to Harry and licked his face and hands, and then sat beside the body, and would not leave his side. Richie moved Harry into the barn and laid him out on some straw. He did this as quickly as possible; he did not want Harry's children to see their father like this.

Bernadette was in shock.

'Why? We were getting him out of this. For the past two nights he had been sitting up late writing letters. I didn't realise how bad he must have been feeling. I thought he was just nervous.'

'Writing letters?'

'He wanted to write to some of his relations and friends that he had not seen for years.'

'Perhaps it is my fault. He probably couldn't handle going to America and leaving his farm and Ireland. What have I done?' Richie felt the tears welling up inside him. 'What have I done?' he repeated.

When they had done what they could to present Harry to the family, Bernadette said to give her a few moments alone with him before they went into the home to tell the children.

Richie waited outside in the yard. Was he responsible for this? He tried to concentrate on what needed to be done next. He was shocked.

After what seemed a long time, Bernadette came out of the barn.

'Now,' she said to Richie, 'we need to get the doctor and the police officer to come and review the situation. I will have to keep my wits about me and make sure every-thing is correct and in order. Richie, I will ask you to go and get the doctor and the officer we need to get this done as quickly as possible. I don't want anyone to know what happened here this morning, apart from our children. No one needs to know anyway. Come in for a quick cup of tea; the kettle is on the boil. The children are still in bed.'

Richie could not believe that Bernadette was inter-ested in making cups of tea in this situation. But perhaps it was as good a reaction as any. Confronted by a crisis, she relied on her routine. It was a life of routines they had chosen.

As they turned to head for the kitchen door, the sons were there standing and waiting for Bernadette to say something.

'What happened?'

'Your father has taken his own life.'

She said it just like that.

Neither of them said a word. They walked over to their mother and put their arms around her.

'It will be all right, Mammy. It will be all right. We will be together and we will make it to America.'

'We can't think about that now,' said Bernadette. 'We have to take arrangements for your father first.'

Bernadette walked slowly back to the house with her sons by her side. They rallied around Bernadette, and were helpful and kind to her. Aoife and the baby came up to the kitchen to ask what all the commotion was about. Bernadette sat her down in her father's chair and gave her the news. She knew that it was going to devastate Aoife, who let out a screeching cry, 'Daddy, Daddy, why did you do this? Didn't you know we need you? We can't do any-thing without you. Where is he now?' Aoife shouted and cried.

'Your daddy had an accident … a serious one. He died a few minutes ago. He is in heaven now with his own parents.'

'That's not right,' Aoife said. 'We need him here with us.'

As she cried, Bernadette broke down too. Both women held on to one another.

'He is not ready for anyone to see him yet. Richie is gone to get the doctor and the police. Oh, Jesus, I forgot about the priest.'

The eldest son decided that he would walk into Bruff and get the priest.

'Go ahead, son, and return as soon as you can.'

She got the holy water from the font beside the door, went out to the barn again, and blessed Harry from head to toe with the holy water and said the act of contrition in his ear. 'May the light of heaven be with you, Harry. We will meet again in heaven.'

Bernadette knew that she had to be strong for her family. She could not help but blame Richie and his idea of leaving for America for Harry's death. It had just put too much pressure on the man. But then she thought that it would be worse to stay where they were and be evicted out onto the road with nowhere to go.

As Richie stood outside the house where his family had once lived, he wondered if it was all his own fault. Perhaps they would be better off without him. And then Harry's eldest son approached him, saying that they needed to get the priest. When they found him he was reluctant to come to the house, but they quickly persuaded him. 'You are needed for this family to give the last rites to Bernadette's husband and for his children and grandchild too.'

All the while, Bernadette stayed in the barn with Harry's body. She stood there until Richie got back with the priest. She was anxious to have the last rites for her husband, although she had already said the act of contrition into Harry's ear.

Aoife was still in her room with the baby.

Bernadette decided to wait a while before going back into the house. She did not want to leave Harry unattended to. She would bend down and rub Harry's brow and brush back his hair, gently touching him.

When Richie returned, Bernadette was waiting at the top of the lane. She had heard the car in the distance. When the priest stood out of the car, Bernadette ran to him.

'Father, the most awful thing has happened … my husband, Harry, is dead. We were all getting ready to leave Ireland for America, and now he … then he … now this has happened. What am I going to do?'

'I will anoint him with the holy oils and give him the last rites.'

Bernadette stood beside the priest, repeating silently every word he said over Harry.

'What will we do now? Dad was coming to America with us,' Aoife said.

'When we have the funeral over, we will leave here for a new life,' said Bernadette.

'We can still go, then?' Aoife asked.

'We have to go … we won't have anywhere to go if we stay here. Richie will look after that for us. He will have to cancel our passage and book again for next week instead. I can't … I can't think about those things right now.'

Going back into the house, Bernadette began turning the clocks so they faced the wall. The ticking could be heard, but no time was shown. She covered the mirrors with a black cloth. It was one more ritual.

22.

It wasn't long before the news got around that Harry O'Keeffe was dead. The family kept to themselves that he had killed himself, but people speculated about it just the same. It was seen as a sin, something of which to be ashamed. Harry was laid out on the bed in the parlour on the middle of the floor so that friends and neighbours could sit at each side of the coffin, while other people who came to offer their respects could come and stand and pray and spray holy water from the font with a feather that Bernadette had placed on a small table beside the coffin. When people prayed over the dead body, they reached for the holy water to do the sign of the cross. His neck was not visible; his long white beard covered the marks on it.

Richie began to remember the stories Harry told him about the ghost in the house, and about the story of the hanging of the young woman many years ago. Was history repeating itself? Had Harry been driven mad by some ghostly presence? Richie dismissed the thought from his mind. There were a hundred things weighing upon that poor man's mind, but they were real things caused by real people. One did not cherish the memory of the departed by pretending that their troubles were imaginary ones. Richie knew that Harry's troubles were real enough, and he felt angry. Angry ... and responsible.

Ghost or no ghost, the family would not sleep in that house again, so it scarcely mattered now, he told himself.

On the night when he first came to the O'Keeffes' and slept in the parlour, though, he had found it frightening. Maybe the spirits of people who died who were not ready to die somehow stayed in the world, connected to a place. Who knew such things? If so, this place had to be alive with many souls.

Many a tragedy and untimely death had happened in this house. The local people talked about this unfortunate death, and wondered about the past deaths. Some, many of them older people, said that the place was cursed and that a spirit lived in it. Nothing would change their minds about this, and each new tragedy did nothing to dissuade them from their view. Stories tumbled down from one generation to the next, and were remembered and retold in the early hours in homesteads.

When the undertaker came to see to Harry's remains, he undressed him privately down in the parlour. He folded the clothes Harry was wearing and left them on the settle bed, which was folded up now. He dressed Harry in a blue satin shroud with his hands folded over his chest and the rosary beads intertwined his fingers. He looked peaceful, just like he had fallen asleep. When the undertaker had everything he wanted to do done, he handed Harry's clothes to Bernadette. She took them to their bedroom.

In Harry's pocket Bernadette found his pocket watch. It seemed to have stopped at the time when he died. Or had he stopped it himself, as if to mark the moment in time? She held it in the palm of her hand, then placed it on her chest and said a prayer for Harry. In his other pocket she found his pipe and tobacco, along with a small knife he used to cut the tobacco and clean out the pipe. These objects had been with him for a lifetime. She loved the smell of the tobacco, and would forever associate it with her late husband. His clothes smelled of it—a rich, musky smell of vanilla.

When Bernadette continued to arrange Harry's clothes and things, she came across some notepaper, with a note addressed to each member of the family.

Bern,

If you are reading this, I had the courage to carry out my plan.

I beg your forgiveness for the pain I have caused you and our children. I am so, so sorry. But I could not leave Bruff to live in America. I could not leave our farm. I could not leave my friends, or leave Ireland. If we had stayed, though, we would have ended up being thrown out onto the street, and you mean far too much to me for me to let that happen. I am too old to change, and this is the only way forwards that I can see to get out of this. I am freeing myself, and my family too, in the only way I can see how.

With me out of the way, nothing can stop you moving to America, where you will have the chance to be happy. And God knows you deserve it. You all do. When I think of our new granddaughter, all I want is for her to have a better chance than we have had. That is the most important thing.

I don't know whether to be proud or ashamed of what I am going to do. I will have a better time in heaven than I have had on earth. I love you, I have loved you always, and I hope that I will see you again in a better place.

With my love, always,

Harry.

People from all around Limerick and beyond came to pay their respects to Harry O'Keeffe and his family. The funeral was about to leave the house, when everything went silent. People looked around and made a division in the crowd. Members of the Brotherhood walked through the crowd, dressed in full army attire with rifles by their sides. Moving towards the coffin where Harry lay, they lined up, ten on each side. A command was barked, and the Brotherhood draped the Irish flag, green, white and gold. Their commander said the 'Our Father' in Gaelic. Another command was barked, and the men stood back. Bernadette was presented with the flag. Some of the people got carried away, and began to lift the soldiers as high as possible, carrying them through the crowd. But their commander would not allow this, and order was quickly restored.

This gesture from the Brotherhood was the highest honour anyone could receive. It brought tears to the family's eyes. Richie Fitzgerald felt many things as he saw this ritual performed. He was accepted well enough, but could never truly be a part of this in the way that others were.

People gathered at the graveside, where prayers were said. Just before the coffin was lowered into the ground, the soldiers appeared again. Standing alongside the coffin, they lifted their rifles and fired a volley of five shots. The Last Post was played, and its sound haunted all those who heard it. Almost nobody had expected this to happen, least of all Richie, who had never witnessed such a thing.

Almost nobody. As the mourners made their way out onto the road, they were watched by a group of British soldiers. The members of the Brotherhood, of course, had made themselves scarce and moved off in other directions, separating rather than filing out as a group. As the mourners made their way past the soldiers, avoiding making eye contact, Seanie yelled out, 'That's him! The one who hurt Aoife!'

'Seanie, no!' Brendan shouted out, but he was too late. Seanie was already on top of the man, screaming in fury as he pounded his fists into the Brit's head. Other soldiers went for their guns, and John and Brendan O'Keeffe were on them, fists flying in all directions. Brendan felt the thud of a rifle butt as it hit him in the side of his head. He struggled back to his feet, just in time to hear the shot that blew the side of Seanie's head clean off.

23.

*E*verybody had liked Seanie. The kindness of the people
from Limerick and beyond was unbelievable. Trays of
food, all kinds of sandwiches, big pots of soup and pots
of stew arrived. People who had nothing still shared it.
Everyone who came through the door had something to
eat or drink, as they had when Harry had gone.

The day came for Seanie to be brought to the church.
Mass was said, and Seanie's soul offered up to the Lord.
Then everyone walked behind the family, who walked
behind the coffin. More prayers were said at the graveside, and then the coffin was lowered down into the grave,
Brandon and John helping to lower the ropes. Immediately,
the gravediggers began to shovel earth onto the coffin
while the priest kept praying. 'Ashes to ashes, dust to dust.'
A decade of the rosary was said, and then everyone began
to depart.

Richie walked the family back to his car and took
them back to the family home. He didn't stay for long; he
did not want to intrude upon their grief.

Bernadette called out to him, 'Will you be back tomorrow?'

'Tomorrow or the next day.'

'We will keep our plan to leave here.'

Richie tried to stay out of the way until the O'Keefes were ready for him to get their new tickets.

'I am trying to give them some time,' he said to Tom, the hackney man.

'Ah, you are right there,' he replied. 'They need a bit of time to grieve.'

Richie make arrangements that when the time came to re-book the tickets for the journey, Tom would return and help with the luggage as it would not all fit in the one car with the family.

'Come to think of it,' said Tom, 'what about your car? What will you do with it? Sure, you can't bring it back to America with you?'

'They can transport it back for me.'

'I wonder if I might buy that car from you, Richie,' Tom said.

'Do you have £250 in your pocket? They aren't cheap.'

'Be Jaysus, I don't,' Tom replied. 'Sure I could never make that kind of money, not even in a lifetime here in Bruff.

'I am fond of the car myself. It won't cost that much to ship it. And it could come in handy when we get off at the other end in Boston.'

'Perhaps I will go over to America one day,' said Tom.

'You will be welcome,' said Richie. 'If ever things get really difficult, don't get into the state that Harry did. Write to me instead. I will try to fix you up with work and somewhere to stay.'

'It's just that everyone is leaving here to make a better life for themselves abroad. I have been talking to the missus about that, and she would be in agreement for me to go first, and then when I have enough money I will send home the fare for them. The O'Keeffes were finding it very hard to cope on their own with no money coming in and the landlord hounding them for the rent. They knew that when Harry was gone there was a slim chance they would be paid! Fuckin' animals they are.'

★ ★ ★

By the end of May, the O'Keeffes proclaimed that they were ready to leave Ireland for good and set sail for America. 'The sooner we get there now, the better,' Bernadette said. 'Every day spent in our family home it gets harder to leave. But we must go … otherwise we will be put out.'

On the following Friday morning, their ship was to depart Queenstown for Liverpool. 'We all need to be there two hours before sailing,' Richie told them, 'so I will collect you at five. I will take you and Tom will take your luggage. That way will work better than trying to take everything together.'

None of the O'Keeffes slept for two nights, only little baby Gertrude.

When the day came, they were up and ready hours before Richie said he would collect them. The home looked bare—not that they had much before. But they had the little things, the holy water, the small font, the pictures on the walls and the mirror at the kitchen door. When the pictures were taken down there was a mark of dust the shape and size of the picture, smelling of damp as the fire had been lit for the last two days. The ashes were out on the floor; there was no heat in the house.

On the journey to Queenstown, everyone was quiet in the car. They looked outwards at the trees and the ditches, knowing that they were probably seeing their country for the last time. They all felt that mixture of nervousness and excitement that one does at such times. And the knowledge that they would not see these sights and these places again made the sights and places they had seen so many times now seem beautiful, as if they were seeing them for the first time.

The ship was docked and refuelling for the trip. Many passengers were standing waiting along with the O'Keeffes. The horn sounded, and loading started. Chests were delivered to cabins amongst the noise and chaos.

Passengers crossed the threshold of the ship, never to return to their homes in Ireland.

Passengers stood on the deck as the ship left the port, seeing their homeland becoming smaller as they moved farther away, receding into the distance.

But one passenger did not look back towards her homeland. Bernadette O'Keefe did not join the crowd of people who waved their farewells at those left behind at the docks. She felt that Harry was still with her as she looked towards America, and their future.

— The End —